The
Big
Love

a novel

Sarah Dunn

PENGUIN BOOKS

PENGUIN BOOKS

Published by the Penguin Group
Penguin Books Ltd, 80 Strand, London WC2R 0RL, England
Penguin Group (USA) Inc., 375 Hudson Street, New York, New York 10014, USA
Penguin Books Australia Ltd, 250 Camberwell Road, Camberwell, Victoria 3124, Australia
Penguin Books Canada Ltd, 10 Alcorn Avenue, Toronto, Ontario, Canada M4V 3B2
Penguin Books India (P) Ltd, 11 Community Centre, Panchsheel Park, New Delhi – 110 017, India
Penguin Group (NZ), cnr Airborne and Rosedale Roads, Albany, Auckland 1310, New Zealand
Penguin Books (South Africa) (Pty) Ltd, 24 Sturdee Avenue, Rosebank 2196, South Africa

Penguin Books Ltd, Registered Offices: 80 Strand, London WC2R 0RL, England

www.penguin.com

First published in the United States of America by Little, Brown and Company 2004
First published in Great Britain in Penguin Books 2004

1

The author is grateful for permission to reprint "Like a Rotten Log . . ." from *Japanese Death
Poems* by Yoel Hoffman, courtesy Charles E. Tuttle, Inc., of Boston, Massachusetts, and Tokyo, Japan.

Printed in England by Clays Ltd, St Ives plc

For my parents

Joe and Carolyn
and Pete

And for David

The

Big Love

One

TO BE FAIR TO HIM, THERE IS PROBABLY NO WAY THAT TOM could have left that would have made me happy. As it turns out, I'm in no mood to be fair to him, but I will do my best to be accurate. It was the last weekend in September. We were having a dinner party. Our guests were about to arrive. I ran out of Dijon mustard, which I needed for the sauce for the chicken, and so I sent my boyfriend, Tom — my "live-in" boyfriend, Tom, as my mother always called him — off to the grocery store to get some. "Don't get the spicy kind," was, I'm pretty sure, what I said to him right before he left, because one of the people coming over was my best friend, Bonnie, who happened to be seven months pregnant at the time, and spicy food makes Bonnie sweat even more than usual, and I figured that the last thing my dinner party needed was an enormous pregnant woman with a case of the flop sweats. It turned out, though, that that was not the last thing my dinner party needed. The last thing my dinner party needed was what actually happened: an hour after he left, Tom called from a pay phone to tell me to go ahead without him, he wasn't coming back, he didn't have the mustard, and oh, by the way, he was in love with somebody else.

And we had company! I was raised in such a way that you didn't do anything weird or impolite or even remotely human when you had company, which is the only way I can explain what I did next. I calmly poked my head into the living room and said, "Bonnie, can you come into the kitchen for a second?"

Bonnie waddled into the kitchen.

"Where's Tom?" Bonnie said.

"He's not coming," I said.

"Why not?" she said.

"I don't know," I said.

"What do you mean, you don't know?"

"He said he's not coming home. I think he just broke up with me."

"*Over the phone?* That's impossible," Bonnie said. "What were his exact words?"

I told her.

"Oh my God, he said that?" she said. "Are you sure?"

I burst into tears.

"Well, that is completely unacceptable," Bonnie said. She hugged me hard. "It's unforgivable."

And it was unforgivable, truly it was. What made it unforgivable, as far as I was concerned, was not merely that Tom had ended a four-year-long relationship with no warning, or that he had done so over the telephone, or even that he had done it in the middle of a dinner party, but also this: the man had hung up before I had a chance to say so much as a single word in reply. That, it seemed to me, was almost inconceivable. What made it unforgivable as far as Bonnie was concerned was that she was sure the whole thing was nothing more than a ploy of Tom's to keep from having to propose to me anytime soon. She actually articulated this theory while we were still hugging, thinking it would calm me down. "Men are trying to *avoid* getting married," Bonnie said to me. "It doesn't look fun to them." She stroked my hair. "Their friends who are married look *beaten down*."

As if on cue, Bonnie's husband Larry walked into the kitchen with a striped dishrag tucked into the waistband of his pants, carrying two plates of chicken marsala. Larry was very proud of his work with the chicken. When Tom hadn't shown up on time with the mustard, Larry came up with the marsala concept, and made it by picking the mushrooms out of the salad. One thing I will tell you about Larry is that he cheated on Bonnie when they were dating, he cheated on her left and right in fact, but now here he was, father of two, maker of chicken marsala, the very picture of domestic tranquillity. He was beaten down, maybe; but he was beaten down and faithful.

"Tom's not coming," Bonnie said to Larry. "He says he's in love with somebody else."

"Who is he in love with?" Larry asked.

I knew who he was in love with, of course. I hadn't even bothered to ask. He was in love with Kate Pearce. And I knew it! I *knew* it! Bonnie knew it too — I could tell by the look on her face. Bonnie and I had been conferring on the subject of Tom's old college girlfriend Kate for quite some time, actually — ever since she had invited Tom out for the first of what would turn out to be a series of friendly little lunches, an event which incidentally happened to coincide with Bonnie's acquisition of a Hands Free telephone headset. I mention the Hands Free telephone headset only because once she got it, pretty much all Bonnie wanted to do was talk on the phone.

"Tom started doing sit-ups last night during *Nightline*," I told Bonnie during one of our phone calls. "Do you think that means anything?"

"Probably not," Bonnie said.

"I don't think a person all of a sudden starts doing sit-ups one day for no reason," I said.

"A few weeks ago *Rocky* was on TNT, and the next day Larry set up his weight-lifting bench in the garage, so it could be nothing."

"Did he say who?" Larry asked me. He put the chicken marsala down on the kitchen counter. "Did he tell you who he's in love with?"

"He's in love with Kate Pearce," I said. There was something incredibly painful about saying that sentence out loud. I sat down at the kitchen table and quickly amended it: "At least, he thinks he's in love with her."

"It's probably just a fling," said Bonnie.

"Is that allowed?" said Larry.

"Of course it's not allowed," Bonnie said. "I just mean, maybe it'll blow over."

"You've never seen her," I said. "She's beautiful."

"*You're* beautiful," Bonnie said, and then she reached across the table and patted my hand, which had the effect of making me feel not beautiful at all. Nobody ever pats a beautiful person's hand when they tell them that they're beautiful. It's just not necessary.

My friend Cordelia came into the kitchen to see what was going on, and I took one look at her and burst into tears again. Cordelia burst into tears, too, and I got up from the table and we stood there on the gray linoleum for what seemed like forever, hugging each other the way you do when there is a dead relative involved. It wasn't until much later that I found out that Cordelia, at that moment, thought there actually *was* a dead relative involved, and if she had known the true state of affairs she wouldn't have cried nearly as much. She is very philosophical about matters of the heart, philosophical in the way that it's only possible to be if you have been married once already and have absolutely no intention of doing so ever again. Cordelia was married to Richard for just under two years. They had what they deemed the usual problems, so they tried the usual solution: they went into therapy together. In the open, mutually accepting atmosphere fostered by their marriage counselor, Richard confessed to Cordelia that he was into amateur pornography. Cordelia thought, okay, not an ideal situation perhaps, but human sexuality is a complicated thing, and she could keep an open mind about her husband's little peccadilloes. Thus emboldened, Richard went on to make what would turn out to be a pivotal clarification — he was, it turned out, *in* amateur pornography — and Cordelia realized that her mind was not that open.

"Well, he can't break up with you over the phone," Cordelia said, after Bonnie told her what had happened. "You live together. You own a couch together."

"I've never told you this before," Bonnie said to me, "but I've always hated that couch."

"Tom picked it out," I said. This made me start crying again. "I didn't want him to think that moving in with me meant he wouldn't get to pick out couches anymore."

"That couch," Bonnie said to Larry, "is why I don't let you pick out couches."

Shortly after that, Bonnie went out into the living room and sent the rest of the guests home. Then she and Larry cleaned up the kitchen so I wouldn't have to wake up to a big pile of dirty dishes. Then Cordelia tucked me into bed with a bottle of wine. I told them I wanted to be alone, and the three of them finally left.

You should probably know that my first thought after I hung up the phone with Tom was that the thing with the ring was probably a mistake. What had happened was this: some months before, I happened upon a picture of an engagement ring I liked in a magazine, and I'm ashamed to tell you that I cut it out, and I'm even more ashamed to tell you that I did, in fact, slip it into Tom's briefcase while he was in the bathroom taking a shower. I did not expect him to run out the next day and buy the ring. I thought it was information he might want to have on file at some indeterminate time in the future. When Larry asked Bonnie what kind of engagement ring she'd like, she said she didn't want a solitaire, she wanted something different, and he said fine, different, I can do that, and Bonnie had a sudden flash of what he might come up with on his own — Larry being a man who once staple-gunned two old brown towels over his bedroom window and left them hanging there for four years — so she drew a picture on a cocktail napkin of a wide band of channel-set diamonds, and she wrote down the words *platinum* and *size six* and *BIG* and *SOON*. Larry dutifully took the napkin to a jeweler, and now Bonnie has on her finger something that looks like a very sparkly lug nut.

Of course, it's possible I'm putting too much emphasis on the whole business with the ring, but I tend to zero in on one detail and skip over everything else. I always have. I took a life drawing class in college, and at the end of the first two-hour session the only thing I had on my sketchpad was an exquisite rendering of the model's gigantic uncircumcised penis. But, well: *Obviously* I shouldn't have put the picture of that ring in Tom's briefcase. *Obviously* I should have put my foot down about the Kate stuff from the very beginning. I see that all clearly now. It just never entered my mind that Tom would actually have an affair! That's a lie. It entered my mind constantly, but whenever I brought it up Tom would assure me I was being crazy. "I can't live this way," he'd say to me. "If you don't trust me, maybe we should just end this now," he'd say to me. And he'd be so calm and cool and logical that I'd think: He's right, this is my stuff, this is my paranoia, this is happening because my father left when I was five, I was in an Oedipal stage, I have an irrational fear of abandonment, and I need to get over it. And then I'd be hit by a thought like, "Don't crush the sparrow, hold it with an open hand; if it comes back to you it's yours, if it doesn't, it never was." And I'd be fine, in a real Zen state, and then I'd try to re-member where the sparrow thing came from, which would make me think of Antoine de Saint-Exupéry's *The Little Prince* even though there is actually no connection beyond a sort of dippy adolescent obviousness, which would make me think of Tom's most cherished possession — a dippy hand-painted *Little Prince* T-shirt made for him in college by Kate, the same Kate he was busy lunching with — and I'd be right back where I started.

"Listen," I said to Tom during one of our discussions about Kate. "I just don't feel comfortable with you having lunch with your old girlfriend all the time."

"I'm capable of being friends with a person I used to go out with," Tom said. "You're still friends with Gil."

"First of all, I'm not still friends with Gil," I said. "Second of all, Gil is gay, so even if I were still friends with him, it wouldn't count, because he's not interested in having sex with me. When he was having sex with me he wasn't interested in having sex with me."

"Kate has a boyfriend," Tom said. I rolled my eyes. "She and Andre *live* together," he said. I stifled a snort. "I'm not going to have this conversation anymore," he said, and then he left to go play squash.

Not that all this fighting did me any good. He just kept on having lunch with her. He even wanted me to have lunch with her! He gave her my work number and everything. "Kate's going to call you next week. She wants to have lunch with you," he said. I spent an entire weekend mulling over my plan. I decided I wouldn't call her back. I wouldn't answer my phone and when I got her message I'd just never call her back and she'd get the picture and then do you know what happened? She never called! I should have known then what I was dealing with. Not that knowing would have done any good. When a woman like Kate Pearce wants your boyfriend, I don't think there's much you can do to stop it.

I don't mean to make it sound like Tom had no part in this. I warned him. "She doesn't just want to be friends with you," I'd say. "That's not how women like that operate," I'd say. "She's not going to stop until she has sex with you." Tom had even wanted to invite her to our dinner party that night! "She doesn't have many friends," he said. Right, I thought. First I invite her to a dinner party and then she insinuates herself into my circle of friends and the next thing you know she's nailing my boyfriend. I know how these things work, I thought. Unfortunately I didn't know how this particular thing was working, because Kate had skipped the preliminaries. She already was nailing my boyfriend. She'd been doing it for five months!

"We don't have enough chairs for Kate and Andre," I said to Tom when he suggested the dinner party invitation.

"It would just be Kate," Tom said. "And I'll sit on a folding chair."

"What happened to Andre?" I said.

"He's not in the picture anymore," Tom said.

"What do you mean he's not in the picture anymore?" I said.

"They broke up. I thought you knew that."

"How could I possibly know that?"

You're probably wondering, if this affair had been going on for five months, how come Tom hadn't moved out earlier. Which is an excellent question. We weren't married. We didn't have any kids. He could have broken up with me and then moved out and then started seeing Kate and through it all kept his moral compass pointing north. But, as it turned out, Tom hadn't done any of those things in the proper order because *Kate wanted to take it slow!* And he didn't want to scare her off! Like she was a baby deer in a forest clearing or something! The most disturbing part, however, is the *reason* Kate wanted to take things slow. Apparently, Andre's mother was sick, very sick — sick with advanced pancreatic cancer in fact — and Kate didn't think it would be fair to walk out on him in his time of need. So there was Tom, waiting for Andre's mother to die from pancreatic cancer and for a suitable amount of time to pass so that Kate could drop the hatchet on Andre with a clear conscience and then, only then, was he going to get around to breaking up with me. I'm thirty-two years old, people! I don't have that kind of time!

I didn't know any of that stuff the night of the mustard, though. That first night all I really knew for sure was that Tom had been having lunch with his ex-girlfriend all summer and he'd been reading a book of Japanese death poems called *Japa-*

nese Death Poems. If nothing else, the whole death poem thing should have tipped me off. A happy person doesn't read a book of poems about death, particularly poems about death that were written only moments before each poet's actual demise, which is what this book was full of. *Written by Zen Monks and Haiku Poets on the Verge of Death* happens to be the subtitle. Tom would read a bunch of these poems before bed each night and then he wouldn't be in the mood to have sex. Sometimes he'd even read one aloud to me, which at the time I thought was nice — Tom and I were never a read-aloud-to-each-other kind of couple, we were a read-it-when-I'm-done kind of couple — although I now suspect he was only doing it so I wouldn't be in the mood to have sex either. These poems were unbelievably depressing. *Like a rotten log / half-buried in the ground — my life, which / has not flowered, comes / to this sad end.*

Anyhow, I was in bed, flipping through the death poem book, drinking my wine, trying not to think about Tom, or Tom and Kate, and what it was precisely that they did together, and whether or not they were doing it at that very moment, when the phone rang.

My heart leapt.

I let the machine pick it up. It was Nina Peeble, one of the people who'd been in my living room earlier, calling from her cell phone.

"I just want you to remember one thing, Alison," Nina said into the machine. "They *always* come back."

Two

THE LAST THING TOM SAID TO ME BEFORE HE HUNG UP THE phone that night was, "Don't write about this." He thought I might be tempted to take the mustard and the dinner party and the phone call and whip it into seven hundred words and run it as my column for the week. I'd been writing essentially the same column since college, but by the time Tom and I broke up, it was running in an alternative newspaper called the *Philadelphia Times*. The *Philadelphia Times* would like to be the *Village Voice,* only this is Philadelphia, not New York, and that can make it kind of difficult. My friend Eric grew up around here and now lives in Manhattan, and what he says is that Philadelphia is the kind of city where the local newscasters are celebrities. Eric is always saying things like that, things that are true in some obvious and fundamental way and yet nonetheless surprisingly depressing.

Anyhow, as far as not writing about Tom, I really couldn't see how I was going to manage to avoid it. Tom Hathaway was a recurring character in my column, and it simply wouldn't be possible to have him just drop out of it altogether. I was going to have to tell the truth, and there were several general problems with that, and one specific one. First of all, this was not the sort of breakup that reflected well on the victim. I realized that the second I hung up the phone. In fact, it strikes me that if I hadn't had a living room full of witnesses, it's entirely possible I would have changed the story around a little — made Tom's behavior seem slightly less appalling — not because I wanted to protect him, but because I wanted to protect me. Also, there was the question that always comes up in a situation like this, the what was she (me) doing with him (Tom) in the first place question. Too many pieces of the puzzle were missing, and if that much was clear to me — the person who had been living in the midst of all the puzzle pieces and yet apparently missing them entirely — I could just imagine how it would look to somebody from the outside. So those were the general problems. The specific problem was this: Tom is an attorney, and it crossed my mind that if I wrote about what happened that night when he asked me not to, I might end up getting sued. In my experience, there is a certain type of writer who wastes a lot of energy worrying about getting sued, and usually it's just self-aggrandizing nonsense, but the truth is in this case I'm not so sure. I suppose it doesn't help that I always give people the same names they have in real life. I can't help it. Otherwise I can't keep everybody straight. I really don't believe in changing details much, either. That's what the writing books always tell you to do — "change the identifying details" is how they put it — but I can never bring myself to do it.

I feel I should point out that I became the kind of columnist I became before it was a cliché, before the *Suddenly-Susan*ness of it all hit the culture full force, before the whole thing became boring, and silly, and obvious. By the time all that happened, it was too late. I was hooked. I suppose if I had been exposed to Dorothy Parker at an impressionable age she would have been who I wanted to grow up to be, but we didn't get Dorothy Parker in Arizona when I was growing up; we got Nora Ephron. Who I proceeded to want to grow up to be. I didn't find out until years later — after I'd been exposed to Dorothy Parker myself and had begun to idly contemplate attempting to become her — that Nora Ephron had wanted to grow up to be Dorothy Parker, which made me quite pleased.

Unfortunately, it's very difficult for somebody like me to become somebody like Dorothy Parker, or somebody like Nora Ephron for that matter, because I'm not Jewish. Not only am I not Jewish, I am the opposite of Jewish. I was raised as an evangelical Christian, a real born-again, a tribe which completely lacks a comedic tradition and is almost entirely missing an intellectual one. We also don't have much in the way of a self-hating tradition, come to think of it, although God knows everybody else in the world wishes we would hurry up and develop one. Because — and I realize I don't have to tell you this — people hate evangelical Christians. They hate, hate, hate them. They hate the Christian right, they hate the Moral Majority, they hate Jerry Falwell, they hate the pro-lifers, they hate people with the little silver fish on the back of their minivans, they hate the guy at the office with the weird haircut who won't put money into the football pool. Of course, the guy at the office with the weird haircut could be a Mormon, but for some reason people don't hate Mormons. Most people think of Mormons as just sort of inoffensive super-Christians. The only people who don't think of Mormons as Christians, in fact, are Mormons and Christians. A few years ago, my mother called me and told me that the people who'd moved in next door were Mormons.

"Do they have a trampoline?" I said.

"How did you know?" said my mother.

"Mormons love trampolines," I said. "I don't know why, but they do."

Anyhow, my mother befriended her counterpart next door, and the two of them spent the next three years swapping one-dish recipes and trying in vain to convert one another. Which brings us to people's fundamental problem with born-again Christians, which is that they don't want to be converted. They don't even want to entertain the notion that they might need to be converted. The problem is that at some point in the conversation, the person being converted is going to say something like, "What happens if I decide to take a pass?" and the person doing the converting will get a drippy, painfully sincere look on his face and say, "Then you'll spend eternity in hell." This is upsetting, even if you think they're completely full of shit. And, well, the rest of it sure doesn't look like any fun. Even when I was a kid I knew it wasn't any fun. In high school youth group, no matter what we were doing some kid would say, "See, we don't need to *drink* to have *fun*" — even then I suspected what I now know is true — namely, that it is more fun to drink and do drugs and have sex than to not do so. It is much more fun.

You're probably wondering, if I was an evangelical Christian, what I was doing living with my boyfriend Tom in the first place. Well, the truth is I haven't been much of a Christian for quite some time — since college, really, although some of the more glaring aftereffects lingered well into my twenties, the pink sweaters, the bad hair. If I'd stopped to give the matter any thought I would have jumped ship before I got to college, because being an evangelical Christian in college is unbelievably tedious. Everybody around you is busy drinking and smoking and trying psychedelic mushrooms and experimenting with lesbianism and sucking Jell-O shots out of the navels of strangers in Cancún during spring break, while you sit around, trying to be good. The worst possible thing to be is an evangelical Christian at an Ivy League university — which is what I was — because you're not only trying to be good, you're trying to be smart. You end up fighting the Scopes Monkey Trial over and over again on your dorm room floor — only guess whose side you're on? Guess who you have to be? Plus, there's all that time spent sitting around in small circles with other Christians, pondering imponderable questions. Would it be possible, the classic one goes, for God to make a rock so big that He couldn't lift it? Could He make a black cat that's white? Could He make a square circle? Then you move on to important matters. Like how far you can go and still be considered a virgin. This is a matter of contentious debate, but let me assure you: it is all true about Christian girls and blowjobs. (It is not, however, true about Christian girls and anal sex, with a few truly pioneering exceptions, only one of whom I happen to have met.)

It strikes me that a bit of clarification is in order, and that is that there is no real halfway with evangelical Christianity. Blowjobs notwithstanding. It is possible, for example, to be raised as a Catholic and then to grow up and stop obeying the rules and stop going to church and generally have nothing in your life that would remotely indicate to any reasonable human being that you are a Catholic, and yet still be considered, by yourself and everybody else, a Catholic. Not so with evangelicalism. You're either in or you're out. You're either with them or against them. And so, before we go any further here, I would like to make the point that I am currently out. Another point I'd like to make is that this is just the sort of thing I found really irritating about evangelicalism in the first place.

I hate going on record with that sort of thing, because of my parents. My poor parents. My kind, good, devoutly Christian parents. They really did nothing to deserve this. I mean, I've been in therapy for eleven years, so presumably they did *something* to deserve *something,* just nothing to deserve this. I hesitate to mention my eleven years of psychotherapy, because you'll undoubtedly think I'm really screwed up. The question of how a person with normal-sized problems can end up in therapy for eleven years is one that only a person with nothing much wrong with them who's been in therapy for a long time can understand, so there's really no use in me trying to explain myself here. The more interesting question is how I managed to afford it. Well, when I graduated from college I was broke and depressed and I started going to a public clinic where they only charged me thirteen dollars a session, and before I knew it eleven years had gone by. I didn't make much progress, mainly because it was a teaching clinic where graduate students worked for a year before heading off into private practice, which meant that every September, my current therapist would hand over my file to the new guy, and the two of us would have to start all over again, at the beginning, with my childhood.

There is really no need for you to try to keep all of my therapists straight. There have simply been too many of them. My most recent therapist was named William, and he had vertigo. I for one had always suspected that vertigo was a made-up condition, the sort of thing moviemakers come up with to explain why the hero can't cross the bridge to save the girl, but William had actual vertigo. It got so bad that during our sessions he'd sort of worm down out of his chair and lie down on the floor at my feet. "Go on," he would say. "I'm just having one of my attacks."

"Maybe I should go," I said the first time this happened.

"Why should you go?" said William. He was staring up at me from the carpet. "Does this make you uncomfortable?"

"Yes," I said.

"Why are you uncomfortable?" said William.

"Because my shrink is lying on the floor," I said.

"My lying on the floor is a reasonable response to my attack of vertigo," said William. "Why should that make you uncomfortable?"

"I don't know," I said. "It just does."

"Does it trigger any sexual feelings in you?" said William.

"None whatsoever."

"I find that hard to believe," he said.

"And why is that?"

"Because you are attracted to unavailable men, men like Tom, who even though he is your boyfriend is emotionally unavailable to you, and I as your therapist am by definition unavailable." All of this from the floor.

"You don't seem that unavailable, William."

"Do you mean you think I have sexual feelings for you?"

"I didn't say that," I said.

"Well, I do," he said. "Shall we explore them?"

I should of course have stopped seeing William, but I didn't. You have to keep in mind that I was paying only thirteen dollars a session, and for thirteen dollars a session I was willing to put up with a certain amount of unconventional behavior on the part of my therapist. And I didn't want to make any waves at the clinic, because if anybody ever really examined my file, they'd figure out pretty quickly that they should raise my fee. Which is, unfortunately, exactly what happened approximately three weeks before the night of the dinner party. When I showed up for my regular Monday morning appointment, the director of the clinic poked her head into the waiting room and ushered me back to her office. She sat me down in front of her desk and calmly informed me that William wouldn't be working at the clinic anymore. He'd had to be carted off to the loony bin in a straitjacket and everything, although the director didn't tell me that part, Yolanda the receptionist did. Apparently it was quite a scene. Anyhow, it turned out that I was the only one of William's patients who hadn't complained about him, which is how come I'd ended up in this woman's office. She figured I must have some sort of problem. Of course, everybody at the clinic had problems, she just figured I must have really BIG problems.

All of which is to make the simple point that, although I had been in therapy for just over eleven years, I did not, at the time of the events in question — the events that make up this story — have a therapist. Nor, I might add, was I fixed. I did, however, have a certain affinity for, and interest in, and familiarity with the inner self. Which is why, now that I stop to think about it, the fact that all of this came as such a surprise came as such a surprise. I mean, eleven years of psychotherapy! A father who left when I was five! You don't even have to dig that deep to get at my subconscious — it's all right out there in my life, masquerading as fate. The truth is, I could draw diagrams of why what happened with me and Tom happened; I just haven't been able to figure out how you get from understanding *why* the bad things that are happening to you are happening to the point where you manage to avoid them altogether. That's the part that eludes me at every turn. That's the part I've never been able to get a straight answer on, not from any of my therapists. I actually put the question to Janis Finkle — my last real therapist, the one who immediately preceded William — at our final session, and she said to me, "You don't."

"You don't?" I said.

"You don't," said Janis.

"Then what's the point?"

"What do you think the point is?" said Janis.

Well, I haven't figured out what the point is. Another thing I haven't been able to figure out is whether the religion of my childhood is the source of my neurotic problems or the cure for them. I have figured out a few things, of course, but for the most part, none of them seem to apply.

Three

LATE THAT SUNDAY NIGHT, MY DOORBELL RANG. I HAD SPENT the previous twenty-four hours at home, alone, waiting for just this moment. And I was fully prepared. I had a long speech worked out in my head, a speech that opened with a blanket condemnation of Tom's despicable behavior and segued into a psychological study of all three parties involved and eventually worked itself around to the idea that I loved Tom and he loved me, and we could get through this thing together, with the two-pronged proviso that he agree to see a couples' counselor and promise never to speak to Kate Pearce ever again. It was a pretty good speech, and the truth is I was anxious to try it out. I went over to the front door and peered through the peephole.

"I have something awful to tell you," a man who was not Tom said through the door. "Your boyfriend is having an affair with my girlfriend."

I unhooked the chain and opened the door.

"You must be Andre," I said.

"How did you know?" he said.

"I know all about Tom and Kate," I said, "so I figured you must be Andre."

There were several things about Andre's appearance on my doorstep that made me feel better, but the most obvious was that he was so clearly in worse shape than I was. I'm not talking about what he was wearing (a green tracksuit), or the fact that he obviously hadn't shaved in some time — rather, that Andre's going to the trouble of tracking me down and knocking on my front door was so plainly an act of complete and utter desperation that I felt relatively sane in comparison. I let him in, and we sat down at the kitchen table and immediately started in on a bottle of Tom's good scotch.

"Tell me everything you know," Andre said. "And then I'll tell you everything I know."

I didn't know much. Actually, the only thing I really knew was that Tom and Kate had been having lunch together, and Andre just nodded his head impassively at that, because he already knew about the lunches. Andre, it turned out, knew everything. He'd been spying on the two of them for months — for five months, to be precise, which is exactly as long as the affair had been going on — and whatever he hadn't been able to figure out by spying, Kate had told him outright when she'd finally broken up with him four days before. She'd wanted him to move out of their apartment, and Andre had stubbornly refused to budge — believing, or so he told me, that they could work things out as long as they didn't do anything drastic — so she recounted humiliating detail after humiliating detail about her affair with Tom, hoping, I suppose, to appeal to his sense of pride. I'd only known Andre for about fifteen minutes, but I had a sense that appealing to his pride was the wrong approach.

"And then when she realized I wasn't going anywhere, she finally left," Andre said.

"Where did she go?" I said.

"That's one of the things I thought you might know," he said.

"Well, I don't," I said. "And I don't see how knowing that would do either of us any good."

Andre just looked at me like I was utterly and hopelessly naive. Clearly it would be necessary to ascertain Kate and Tom's whereabouts if he were to continue spying on them.

"Why do you want her back so badly?" I said.

He took a deep breath. "She's like a drug."

"Wonderful," I said.

"I can't get enough of her," he said.

We just sat there a moment, Andre with a lovesick look on his face, and just when I was about to suggest that it might be time for him to leave, he turned to me and asked what Tom was like in bed.

"I'm not going to tell you that," I said.

"Come on," Andre said. "I need to know what I'm up against."

"I don't think how anyone is or isn't in bed is what this is about."

Andre stared at me blankly. "Then what do you think it's about?" he said.

"I think Tom's going through a stage, and he needs to figure some things out."

"Really?" said Andre.

"Yes. And I'm not going to overreact," I said.

"You're very together, you know," Andre said. "You seem like a very together person."

"Thank you."

"And you're nice, too," he said, nodding his head thoughtfully.

"Thank you."

We sat in silence for a moment.

"My mother is dying. She has cancer of the pancreas," he said matter-of-factly, and then he reached across the kitchen table and took hold of my hand.

Now, this made for an awkward moment. I couldn't tell if we were holding hands because Andre's mother was dying of pancreatic cancer, or because our lovers had left us, or because we were both drunk. I gently pulled my hand away.

"I'm sorry," said Andre.

"It's okay," I said.

I swirled the scotch around in my glass with my liberated hand.

"I guess you could be right," Andre said. "It could just be a phase."

"I think it's a stage," I said, "not a phase."

"What's the difference?" Andre said.

"A stage implies growth," I said. "You go through a stage, you come out the other end up a level."

"And a phase is what, then, just nailing some stranger?"

"Yes, and like I said, I don't think that's what this is about."

"Well, it doesn't really matter anyway. Now that we both know about it, it won't last much longer," Andre said.

"Why do you say that?"

"She'll get bored with him," he said. "And then she'll kick the shit out of him. And then you'll get him back."

This wasn't exactly how I pictured Tom coming back to me — brokenhearted, tail between his legs, shit kicked out of him by his demon lover — but it would do. It would have to. *I love him,* I thought.

"I love her," Andre said. It sounded much worse when he said it than when I thought it. "I can't help myself."

"Ninety-five percent of happiness," I said, "is picking the right person to love."

"What's the other five percent?" said Andre.

"That I don't know."

Andre eventually left, but not before giving me his card and taking down my phone number and making me swear to alert him if I found out any new information and promising to alert me if he found out any new information. I didn't see how new information was going to do me any good, especially since the information I had just received was more than enough to send me right over the edge. I mean, if there's one thing I know about a woman who is like a drug, it's that she's better in bed than I am. Not that Tom and I had any major problems in that department, it's just that I've come up with my own definition of great sex as being sex without any need for discussion, and sex without discussion is pretty much impossible for me. *Anything* without discussion is pretty much impossible for me. Sometimes I wish I could be one of those people I see walking down the street who appear to have no inner world whatsoever — although it's certainly possible that these people have inner worlds, I suppose that one of the definitions of an inner world is that it is not apparent to others when they see you walking down the street — but you know the sort of people I mean. People who manage to go through life without *thinking* about everything all the time.

I know that when something like this happens to you, when your boyfriend or husband leaves you because he's been having an affair with another woman, you're supposed to say something like, "It's not the sex that bothers me, it's the lying"; but the truth is that in my case it was the sex. I was always very clear on that. Getting all worked up about the lying seemed altogether beside the point. Even after Andre left and I started piecing things together, reconstructing various lies Tom told me about late nights at work and six-hour Saturday afternoon squash tournaments and weekend business trips — all of that was never anything more than an intellectual exercise, a masochistic one to be sure, but still. The part that really got to me, the part that woke me out of a dead sleep, was always Tom and Kate together, Tom and Kate having sex. I thought about it constantly. I'd picture me coming home early from work, unlocking the front door, walking up the stairs, unlocking the door to our apartment, putting my purse on the hall table, kicking off my shoes, walking into the bedroom, and catching them having sex. I'd make a little yelp of surprise and then I'd run away, down the stairs and out the front door, because it seemed like what one would do in such a circumstance, but also because I wanted to see if Tom would chase me. I wanted to see if Tom, in my fantasy, would at least have the common decency to get off bed and wrap a towel around his waist and chase me out the front door yelling, "Jesus, Alison! This is not as bad as it looks!" I played this scenario over in my head so many times that I eventually stopped running away; I'd just walk in and stand in the doorway and shoot them a look of cool disgust, just like Gwyneth Paltrow in *Sliding Doors,* so much like Gwyneth Paltrow in *Sliding Doors,* now that I think about it, that I'm pretty sure I stole the whole thing outright. Even so, I considered that progress.

I realize I'm in danger of attributing too much importance to sex, if that is possible (which I secretly doubt — but perhaps that's only because I attribute too much importance to it). I've always thought that if I'd had a little more experience in that particular area, if I'd slept with more people, I'd be better off. I'd have more points of reference. I didn't, though. I worry about telling you how many people I'd slept with, so I'll just put it at less than five. More than one, less than five.

And not four or three.

ह●

Part of the problem was that I lost my virginity late, absurdly late really — I was twenty-five, which I think you'll agree puts me at the freakish end of things — and I probably wouldn't even have done it then if it weren't for my therapist, who talked me into it.

"When did you make this decision?" said Celeste, my therapist at the time, when I finally broke down and told her.

"When I was thirteen. I was at church camp. I made a pledge," I said.

"To whom?" said Celeste.

"What do you mean, to whom?"

"To whom did you make this pledge?"

"To God."

"To God," Celeste repeated, and made a little scribble on her yellow legal pad.

My belief in God was one of the things Celeste was attempting to rid me of. Well, that's not entirely fair: she didn't have a problem with my believing in God, she just didn't want it to interfere with anything important, like my freedom or my choices or my sex life. Of course, that's pretty much the whole point of God. You give up some of life's more interesting perks and in exchange you lose your fear of death.

"A decision that served you well at age thirteen, might, at age twenty-five, be subject to reevaluation," said Celeste.

So, we reevaluated. We went around and around. Celeste compared it to the embargo on Cuban cigars. It made a certain amount of sense in the sixties, but now? With the crumbling of the Berlin Wall? A McDonald's in Red Square? To be totally honest, I didn't need much in the way of convincing. I'd been toying with the idea myself ever since Lance Bateman put his hand in my pants in the eleventh grade, but I'd managed to hold off. For a long time I was waiting for my wedding night, and then when that started to seem silly and futile and quasidelusional, for some reason I kept on waiting. I guess I was waiting for a good enough reason to stop waiting.

That night I went over to see my boyfriend Gil-the-homosexual and I told him that I was finally ready to have sex with him. The penis embargo was over. I said I had discussed it with my therapist, and a decision that worked for me when I was thirteen might not make the most sense for me now that I was twenty-five, and since he was my boyfriend he was the logical candidate for the deflowering. I'd even bought a twelve-pack of condoms on the way over, figuring that upon hearing the news he'd throw me down on the kitchen floor and have his manly way with me, maybe not twelve times, but definitely more than three, which was the only other denomination that condoms came in. Gil, however, did not throw me down on the kitchen floor. He just sat there, polishing his shoes with a new soft-bristle toothbrush, and told me he needed some time to think about it. He wasn't sure he was completely on board.

I would like to report that I broke up with him right then and there, that I said something withering and cruel and never looked back, but I didn't. I had a job for the man to do. I'm very practical that way. I'm not the type to throw away a perfectly good blender just because you've got to jiggle the cord a little to get it started. The idea of starting over completely from scratch, of meeting someone new and going out with him once and then twice and then three times and then telling him about my sexual status and watching him slowly back out of the room, explaining that he wasn't interested in getting involved in anything serious and, let's face it, having sex with a twenty-five-year-old virgin is nothing if not serious — that was more than I could bear. So after some jiggling of the cord, Gil-the-homosexual and I had sex, and then not only did I not break up with him, I stayed with him for eight more months, my brain addled not by the sex — the word *perfunctory* applies — but by the thought that now that I'd slept with him I had to marry him.

I did not know at the time we were dating that Gil-the-homosexual was in fact gay. I mean, I had my suspicions — you should have seen the man make a bed — but I did my best to ignore them, largely because I was so relieved to have met somebody who was willing to be my boyfriend without having sex with me. You can't imagine what a find this was. We'd go out about three times a week, and then I'd go sleep over at his place, and we'd make out and cuddle and fall asleep, and the second my feet touched the floor in the morning he'd start in on the bed. He'd pile the pillows and the shams and the bolsters with such precision and flair that it looked like one of those department store beds that you're not supposed to sit on. That's another thing — he didn't like for me to sit on it once it was made. Not even if I needed to put on my shoes. He also made me drink out of paper cups at night because he claimed he couldn't fall asleep if there were dirty dishes in his sink. I myself have been known to fall asleep when there were dirty dishes in my bed. Let's just say, it became a point of contention.

That's one of the things that happens when you wait so long

to have sex: you end up dating men who aren't all that interested in having it. With you, anyway. And then, if you're a certain kind of girl, you end up marrying one of them, and he still isn't all that interested, only now you're stuck with him because he's your husband. You do things the right way, by the letter of the law, and then in the end you get totally fucked. That's one of the things they don't tell you at church camp. That, and the fact that all this pledging never to have sex gives you hang-ups. I'll tell you how big my hang-ups are: I'm not even in my own sex fantasies. And by this I don't mean to suggest that I'm, say, sitting in the corner in an overstuffed armchair smoking a cigarette and watching — I'm not even in the room! I'm someplace else entirely! Quite possibly shopping! And the truth is, the incredibly sad, pathetic truth is, I'm lucky I can even manage to have any sort of sex fantasies at all. It seems to me that most people's really juicy sex fantasies have their roots in adolescent obsessions, and my adolescent obsession was Jesus, and even I am not screwed up enough to have a sex fantasy about Jesus.

I started out telling you all of this because I wanted you to understand why sexual confidence wasn't exactly my strong point, and why Kate being like a drug was precisely the thing that would drive me the most out of my mind with jealousy, but you should also probably know that as upset as I was about Tom leaving me for Kate, the thought did cross my mind that I might finally get to have sex with somebody who a) wasn't Tom, and b) isn't gay. And the prospect didn't entirely lack appeal.

Four

WHEN I WOKE UP ON MONDAY MORNING, I FOUND MYSELF staring up at the pattern on the pressed-tin ceiling over the bed, wondering what would become of me. And I mean this in the full Jane Austen sense of the term. What on earth would *become of* me? When Gil-the-homosexual and I finally broke up — over a ring my Diet Coke made on one of his cherrywood night-stands — I went straight out the next morning and bought a cheap ticket to Prague. I rented a tiny apartment in the Old Town and stayed there for three months. I felt dizzy with my own independence. I was finally free. I drank Turkish coffee and read thick Penguin Classics and took long, soulful walks over bridges. Well, here I was, free again, and all I could think about was Tom. I started to cry. What if he didn't come to his senses? What if he never came back? What would I do? Who would I date? *What would become of me?*

Four years we'd been together. Four years! Well, it's better than a divorce is what you're probably thinking. That's what everybody kept saying to me. At least it's not a divorce. It's better than a divorce. And I would say this back to them. I would say, I'm not so sure about that. A divorced woman at least makes sense to people. A divorced woman has only been rejected by one other human being. Dating a divorced woman is like getting a sweater that's been hanging in someone else's closet; it didn't work for *them,* but maybe . . .

I realize that's nonsense, of course. Cordelia's divorce was truly the most horrific thing I've ever witnessed, and even as I lay there that morning, the picture of misery, mentally tracing the tin bumps on the ceiling in an effort to calm myself down, I knew there was really no comparing the two. Still, all this felt bad, and it was happening to me. Which is one of the reasons it came as such a shock to my system, come to think of it. Very little had happened to me for quite some time. One of the things about living in Philadelphia is that the same events tick along so predictably, year after year, the Mummers Parade and the Flower Show and the Book and the Cook and the Jazz Festival and the Beaux Arts Ball, that you get lulled into a kind of a coma. You see the same faces at the same parties, you're struck by the shock of the same perfect crisp autumn day after the same months of muggy, dank summer, you end up with the same stinky gingko things on the bottom of your shoes when you make the mistake of walking down 22nd Street during gingko fruit season, and after a while you stop noticing that nothing is happening to you, because nothing seems to be happening to anybody else. If anything really big ever happens to anyone who lives in Philadelphia, they end up moving to New York.

One big thing that happened to somebody I knew, about eight months before all this, was that the publisher of our paper, Sid Hirsch, ended up in the news because his wife was found dead in the bottom of his swimming pool. Now, I've always believed that if anybody over the age of about, say, eight, is found dead at the bottom of a swimming pool, it means they were put there by somebody else, so to have this happen to somebody I actually *knew*, to have my boss's wife turn up dead at the bottom of the swimming pool behind their Bucks County home — well, it was almost more than I could take. I'd even swum in the pool! We all had. Every August, Sid and his wife had a big pool party for the staff of the paper, and one of the earliest lines of conjecture around the office was whether or not this year's party would still be on, and if so, if anybody would actually get in the pool. As it turned out, Sid was officially cleared of any wrongdoing, and he permanently canceled the pool party, two facts which should in no way diminish the cloud of creepiness hovering over him in your mind. I'm sorry Sid's wife is dead, truly I am, but a part of me is almost grateful, because it spares me the bother of having to perform a character assassination on him here.

I sat up in bed. I realized I had stopped crying. The last thing I wanted to do was to sit in bed and think about Sid Hirsch, so I got up and went to the paper.

The *Philadelphia Times* was founded in 1971. It was originally called the *People's Avenger,* and then for a while it was just the

Avenger, but at some point in the eighties Sid decided to give it a more mainstream name in order to attract advertisers. There were still a few writers kicking around from the *Avenger* days, and we'd occasionally publish their diatribes on Third World sweatshops and ozone depletion and racial injustice, but mostly we reviewed things. We reviewed books and we reviewed movies and we reviewed albums. We reviewed plays and we reviewed concerts and we reviewed restaurants. Sometimes I wonder if that's why the voice of my Inner Critic is so loud — too many years spent reviewing things — but the truth is that my Inner Critic sounds just like my mother, so it's probably not fair to blame my job. Anyhow, along with all the reviews, we printed a bunch of columns and local event listings, and a truly excessive amount of reader mail. We ran so many reviews and columns and listings and letters, in fact, that there was very little room left in the paper for actual news. We probably wouldn't have bothered with the news at all if it weren't for Warren Plotkin. Warren had received a National Newspaper Award early on in his career for an eight-part series on teenage welfare mothers that he'd written for the *Philadelphia Daily News*. A week later it surfaced that he'd stolen most of it from a graduate dissertation he'd found online, at which point the *Daily News* fired him, at which point Sid Hirsch took him out to dinner at The Palm and offered him a job as news editor, at two-thirds his *Daily News* pay. We were lucky to have him. We were lucky to have anybody, really, which is not to say that there was nothing to like about working there. The truth is, there were many things I liked about working for the *Times*. Not the pay, and not the prestige, both of which were negligible. But I liked that it was the kind of place where you could bring your dog to the office. Not that I had a dog — I just liked knowing that if I ever decided to get one, I'd be able to bring him to the office. And I liked that I could write pretty much anything I wanted to write and then see it in print a week later, virtually unchanged. This is a very seductive state of affairs for a writer, and the fact that the paper was given away for free in cafés and hair salons and juice bars did little to diminish the pleasure. Most of all, though, I liked that the people who worked there were all a little off-center. They were pot addicts and plagiarists and communists and depressives and alcoholics and neurotics and plain old odd-balls, which meant that the one thing that has always plagued me, the quality that, no matter what I do with my hair, I never seem able to shake — my uptight bourgeois suburban normalness — there, at least, made me stand out.

I walked to work. I always walked to work; I got my best ideas that way. I stopped at the Korean market across the street from the office before I went inside. I picked up the *Daily News* and the *Philadelphia Inquirer* and bought a cup of coffee. I crossed the street, and when I got to the front door, I had to set the papers down on the sidewalk at my feet so I could fish around in my bag for my keys. Just as I was about to open the door I heard a church bell ring, which made me look at my watch, which happened to be on the wrist of the hand that was holding the coffee, and I ended up spilling coffee all over the newspapers I'd put on the ground. I made a quick hop to the left and managed to avoid most of the mess; still, the whole thing almost started me crying all over again. I threw the wet newspapers away, and then I walked up the two flights of stairs and made my way down the long, poorly lit hallway towards the bathroom so I could clean myself off.

Well, there I was, on my way to the bathroom, when I saw the cute guy in the blue shirt. He was walking down the hallway directly towards me, and he had one of those really great walks. I wondered what a cute stranger was doing wandering around in our hallway. Maybe he's lost, I thought. He smiled at me. Maybe he's available, I thought. I smiled back. We passed by each other, and I took about three steps, and then I turned my head and looked over my shoulder at his ass. (To this day, I don't know exactly why I did that. I am not the sort of person who checks out men's asses. I'm not even all that interested in asses, as a physical characteristic on a man I mean — I'd put good shoulders and a nice chest higher on my list of priorities; possibly even a really attractive pair of hands.) Anyhow, just as I was turning my head to check out his ass, at that exact moment, the guy in the blue shirt turned his head to check out *my* ass, and we ended up locking eyes, and I laughed twinklingly and he smiled and nodded his head and we both kept right on walking, not missing a beat. I walked past the kitchen and went into the bathroom and locked the door. I did my best with the coffee stains, and then I climbed up on the toilet seat and turned around so I could see my butt in the mirror over the sink. I realized that the cut of my pants made it appear deceptively small (a triumph!), and then I climbed down off the toilet and unlocked the door and headed off to see if I could find out who he was.

I shared an office with Matt, the music editor, and Olivia, the sex columnist. When I walked in, Olivia was at her desk, sorting through a big pile of mail from her readers. She picked up a letter written on pale blue stationery and fluttered it open and began to read it out loud.

"Dear Olivia. After months of ashtanga yoga, I have managed to develop enough flexibility in my spine and neck to be able to gratify myself orally. While understandably pleased with this development, I am worried about sexually transmitted diseases and want to know if it is possible for a person to get AIDS from themselves."

Olivia looked up at me and tilted her head expectantly.

"Something is seriously wrong with the state of public health education in this country," I said.

"You think?" she said.

Olivia's column generally works like this. Philadelphians with various perversions and fetishes and sexual peculiarities send in letters describing in painstaking detail what it is exactly that turns them on. Then they ask her whether they are normal or not. Then she assures them that they are. Once, a woman wrote in saying that she liked to have sex with her German shepherd, and she wanted to know if that was okay. Well, Olivia (who by the way is bisexual) finally came out on the side of decency and morality and restraint and said that having sex with one's dog was definitely *not* okay, because — and you could really hear Olivia's wild, anything-goes, I'll-fuck-anything-on-two-legs mind churning away, because even Olivia had to know that her arbitrary "two legs" standard wasn't going to be compelling enough to make this lady give up her new hobby — *because the dog could not consent.* That is the sort of newspaper the *Times* is. The sort that counsels against bestiality on the grounds that the animal involved can't articulate the word *no.*

(Anyhow, just try to be an evangelical Christian, however nominal, however far in the distant past, and work at an alternative newspaper if you want to get an idea of what it would have been like to be a Jew working for the Nazi High Command. I mean, you have to hide it. You have to hide it *well.* Fortunately, it's not the sort of thing that tends to come up in normal conversation. But what would happen is that, say, Sid Hirsch would ask me what my father did for a living. Well, one of my fathers is an extremely right-wing Republican entrepreneur who is always doing extremely right-wing things like going to prayer breakfasts with John Ashcroft and attempting to privatize the state prisons in Texas. My other father runs the ministry of a famous evangelical Christian quadriplegic who paints with her mouth and types inspirational books with a stick and sings Jesus songs at Billy Graham crusades. So: "He's a dentist" is what I would say.)

Matt swung open the door. He stopped in the doorway with a big grin on his face and a magazine rolled up under his arm. "I just lost twelve pounds. Ask me how."

"Jesus, Matt. Is that my magazine?" said Olivia.

Matt looked down at the copy of *Entertainment Weekly* under his arm like he was noticing it for the first time. "Maybe."

"Keep it," said Olivia.

"Psycho Bathroom Guy was stuck inside," Matt said. He flopped down on the couch. "I saved him from another day trapped in the bathroom."

Psycho Bathroom Guy worked in the advertising department down the hall. He had a phobia about touching the bathroom door, although it took the three of us quite a long time to finally come to that conclusion. For a long time, he was just Loitering Bathroom Guy.

"No matter how big my problems are," Matt said, "at least I am capable of touching a men's room door."

"Yes," Olivia said flatly. "That's something to cling to."

"Ask me about my date," Matt said to me.

"How was your date?" I said.

"I'll skip the boring parts," said Matt. He paused for a moment. "So we're back at her apartment. And she's got two cats. And we're making out on the couch, and I hear a big crash coming from the kitchen. She doesn't want me to investigate. I, of course, insist. Guess what I find in the kitchen."

"What?" I said.

"Two more cats," he said.

"I don't get it," I said.

"She has four cats. But she doesn't want to be The Girl with Four Cats, so she locks two of them in the kitchen whenever a guy comes over. Which makes her just The Girl with Two Cats, which is in itself so unremarkable it doesn't even necessitate classification."

"Why doesn't she just lock all four of them in there and be The Girl with No Cats?" Olivia said.

"That's the brilliant part," said Matt. "She can't, because of the smell."

Olivia nodded her head, appreciating this.

"Are you going out with her again?" I said.

"Of course I'm going out with her again. The woman has demonstrated a level of deviousness I have to respect," said Matt. "If nothing else, I might learn something from her."

Just as I was about to ask if either of them knew anything about the guy in the blue shirt, Sid Hirsch appeared in the doorway.

"Conference room in five minutes," said Sid.

"What is it?" I said.

"Big stuff, people," Sid said. He pounded the doorjamb with his fist three times. "Big stuff."

I feel kind of bad dragging Jeffrey Greene into this story, and I'd leave out what happened to him if I could, but I can't. I always loved Jeffrey. Everyone did. He was the managing editor of the paper, and he'd remained firmly rooted in that post for eighteen years. He was kind and intelligent, sweetly and contentedly gay, and orderly to the point where if you told me he had to lick the light switch three times before he turned it off, I'd believe you. Jeffrey Greene was the person who hired me, in fact — not Sid. When I came back from Prague, I sent Jeffrey some old columns

I'd written for my college newspaper, and he called me in for an interview. In the middle of our meeting, Sid walked by Jeffrey's office and stood in the hallway outside the open door. He looked in at me and said, "Man, can you write." And then he disappeared. I liked Sid for a long time after that, that single compliment garnered him an enormous amount of goodwill, and even though he went on to act like a buffoon and a blowhard and an idiot, for years I believed that deep down he was perceptive and amusing and smart. And then I didn't. And then I started hating him like everybody else. It was a relief to finally hate Sid wholeheartedly. It was a nice pure emotion, sharp black and white in a world of gray. Anyhow, everyone at the paper had been waiting for Sid to do something really off-the-charts horrible for a long time, something worse than simply underpaying us and belittling us and refusing to turn on the air conditioning until June twenty-first and making us put fifty cents in a shoebox every time we wanted a cup of his coffee, and here he'd finally gone and done it: he'd fired Jeffrey Greene.

I found out about it at the staff meeting. We all did. It was quite a shock, actually. I mean, *nobody* got fired from the *Philadelphia Times.* This was the place you ended up when you got fired from someplace else. We were all gathered around the conference table, which was really just two old particleboard trestle tables set end to end, when Sid walked in and said quite matter-of-factly, "Jeffrey Greene is no longer with the paper."

Well, one thing you should probably know about Jeffrey is that I'd always wanted his job. I'd wanted his job for four and a half years. Wanting Jeffrey's job, come to think of it, was the closest I'd come to having an actual ambition. Well, that's not entirely true — I had a handful of lofty, unattainable ambitions, but wanting Jeffrey's job was the only one that could be achieved without any extraordinary effort on my part. I was in line for it, for one thing, and the *Times* was the sort of place where being in line for something really counted. It was one of the remnants of the place's hippie past; outsiders and overt power-seekers were considered suspect. And no one else around the office — in line or otherwise — was even remotely qualified for the job. Anyone who'd ever been remotely qualified to take over from Jeffrey had left a long time ago, when it became apparent to them that Jeffrey had no intention of ever leaving. I hadn't left. I'd stayed for four and a half years, waiting for just this opportunity. And here it was. And I was ready.

"We will all miss Jeffrey. We all love Jeffrey," Sid said. "I would like to suggest, however, that one of the reasons we love Jeffrey is because we are fearful of change."

Sid looked straight at me, and for a minute I was afraid he had gotten wind of Tom's departure and was trying to send me some kind of message. I tried to send him a message back. I'm ready for change, I thought, staring straight at him. Bring it on. I felt a little burst of hopefulness. Maybe this is how it's supposed to happen, I thought. Maybe Tom was supposed to leave so that I could focus on my career, and then that thing would happen that sometimes happens when a woman redirects her energy away from her relationship and puts it into her work, namely, that the man (Tom) would suddenly find me interesting again. It all made perfect sense.

"There's someone I'd like you all to meet," said Sid.

Sid opened the door to his office and motioned to someone outside, who turned out to be the cute guy in the blue shirt from the hallway, who turned out to be taking Jeffrey's job. All of this information spilled out so quickly that I had no chance to react, which was a good thing, because while it was only just hitting me that I was apparently not a good editor, I've always known without a doubt that I am not a good actress.

Five

HIS NAME WAS HENRY WICK, AND HE HAD BEEN A WRITER FOR *Rolling Stone* magazine. In fact, that's just how Sid introduced him, as Henry Wick Who Used to Write for *Rolling Stone*. It was disgusting how pleased Sid was with this fact — I mean, Sid had been pleased with himself when he managed to hire a notorious plagiarist who'd been fired by the local *Daily News,* snagging a real writer from *Rolling Stone* made him practically apoplectic. Anyhow, Sid made a big speech about how he had decided it was time for us as an organization to move to the next level, and how Henry was going to help us get there, and had he forgotten to mention that Henry had written for *GQ* and *Details* and had had a feature published in the *New York Times Magazine*? I will say, to his credit, that Henry looked mildly embarrassed throughout the whole thing. I will also say, again to his credit, that when Sid went around the room and introduced

Henry to each of us individually, Henry shook my hand and gave me a big smile and said quite charmingly, "Nice to finally meet you face to face." And then he and Sid locked themselves in the conference room for the rest of the day, presumably plotting how exactly to go about turning the *Philadelphia Times* into *Rolling Stone.*

༚໑

Bonnie took me to the Opera Café for lunch on Wednesday to cheer me up. I needed cheering up. Tom had left me. My career was in the toilet. I'd gotten caught checking out my new boss's ass. And I know there are women who like drama, who create little soap operas just so they can feel like they are the star of their own life, but I am not one of them. In fact, it occurs to me that that was part of the reason I was with Tom in the first place: he didn't go in for drama. If I ever tried to get dramatic, he'd go into the other room.

"Larry and I have someone we want to fix you up with," Bonnie said after we sat down.

"Tom left *five days* ago," I said.

"So?"

"So I'm still *in love* with him," I said.

"That's what makes it so perfect," said Bonnie. "If you're still in love with Tom, it'll be easy for you to act like a normal person. Nothing's at stake for you. You're just having dinner."

You should probably know that six years before all of this happened, Bonnie gave me the telephone number of her cousin Jake, who was working as a management consultant and happened to be passing through Philadelphia. He *claims* I called him eight times. This piece of false information made its way back to Bonnie via a complex communication network consisting of her aunt and her cousins and her mother and her sister Lisa, and as a result Bonnie and her entire extended family are convinced I behave like a mental patient whenever a single man is involved.

"You know how they say you're supposed to act like you're not interested?" Bonnie said. "Well, you won't be acting. You *aren't* interested."

"If I'm not interested, then why am I out on this date?" I said.

"Think of it as practice," she said.

"Wait," I said. "Is this guy a real date or a practice date?"

"If you like him he's real, and if you don't he's practice."

"We've already established I can't like him, because I'm still in love with Tom, so that means he's practice, and the last thing I'm interested in at this point in my life is a practice date," I said.

"You haven't been out there in a while. Dating at thirty-three is different than dating at twenty-eight."

"First of all, I'm thirty-two. Second of all, you got married when you were twelve, so how do you know what dating at thirty-three is like?" I said. "Information I have only a theoretical interest in, seeing as I am thirty-two."

"When you're thirty-two, or thirty-three, basically when the word *thirty* with or without a hyphen can be used to describe you, men think you want to have a baby. They watch the news. They read the papers. They're familiar with escalating rates of mongoloidism. They think, she's nice, but if I start dating her now, in six months she'll be putting the screws to me. If you're twenty-eight, they think there's still breathing room. They're more relaxed, you're more relaxed, everything has a better chance of working out."

"I've got breathing room," I said.

"No you don't."

"Yes I do."

"Alison, you wasted your breathing room on Tom."

Placido Domingo started singing a song from *West Side Story*. Maybe Bonnie's right, I thought. Maybe this isn't just another romantic failure. Maybe this is the one that's going to ruin my life, the one to which all of my future disappointments will be traced — my inability to conceive children, my parents being too old to see my adopted daughter, Ping, graduate from college, the fact that I end up dying unloved and alone. I picked at the goat cheese on my salad. I wondered if I'd have to fly to China to pick up Ping, or if they'd just stick her on a plane and we'd meet up in an airport lounge. I've never really wanted to go to China.

"I'm not saying they're right," Bonnie said. "You have plenty of time. Wendy Wasserstein had a baby when she was forty-eight."

"The last thing I want to do when I'm forty-eight years old is have a baby with some defrosted sperm and my mother holding my hand in the delivery room," I said.

"Your mother will be almost eighty by then," Bonnie said. "Maybe she'll be dead."

"The women in my family live a very long time."

* * *

The women in my family do, in fact, live a very long time. My great-aunt Ellie was still mowing her neighbor's lawn when she was a hundred and seven years old. My grandmother — who everybody calls Grandma Texas even though she lives in Idaho — is ninety-four, and she still drives her 1984 Chrysler LeBaron every day (although as an accommodation to her age she more or less exclusively limits herself to right turns), and she still volunteers at St. Luke's Hospital, even though St. Luke's Hospital is no longer affiliated with the Catholic Church and is owned instead by a large HMO that nonetheless happily lets her run the information desk for three hours every Tuesday morning, for free. I called Grandma Texas a few days after Tom left. I told her what had happened, and at some point I made what I thought was a little joke. What I said was, "Now I'm the family old maid." "Oh, don't be silly," Grandma Texas said, in a kind, grandmotherly tone; "Claire is." Now, it is true that my cousin Claire is thirty-eight years old and not married. It is also true that Claire is a lesbian, although nobody has gotten around to telling Grandma Texas that fact, who thinks that Claire and her roommate, Karen, are just two career girls who are down on their luck in the man department. Claire and Karen have lived together for eleven years, and every December they send out Christmas cards featuring a photo of the two of them hugging some stray dog they found limping around behind an Exxon station, and they both have let themselves go to such an extent that the consensus is that they're incredibly lucky to have one another. It was precisely this line of thinking that made me realize, after I got off the phone with Grandma Texas, that you couldn't really consider Claire an old maid, seeing as she'd found what appeared to be lasting happiness with another human being, which in turn made me face the following fact: I was the family old maid. It was such a depressing thought, really, that I didn't even stop to think how truly idiotic it was. But something happens to a person in a situation like this. At least, something happened to me.

"I'll go out with him," I said to Bonnie when the check came.

"Great. I'll have Larry give him your number."

"What's his name?" I said.

"Bob."

"Bob?"

"Don't start."

"I'm not starting."

"Larry says he's a very nice guy."

"Is there anything I should know?"

"Like what?"

"Is there anything that will cause me to call you up and say I can't believe you didn't mention that?"

"He's starting to lose some of his hair."

I was silent.

"Hey, I wish Larry would go bald," Bonnie said. "Then I could *relax*."

"Is there anything else?" I said.

"No."

"Okay."

We went outside. It was a beautiful day. Bonnie gave me a hug.

"Do yourself a favor, Alison. Don't mention this whole thing with Tom on your date."

"I thought the whole point of this date was that I could act like myself."

"There'll be plenty of time to act like yourself later, if things go well and he likes you," said Bonnie. "Right now you should act like Audrey Hepburn in *Breakfast at Tiffany's*. You know, light. Airy."

Six

BY FRIDAY, IT WAS STARTING TO SEEM A LITTLE STRANGE TO ME that Tom hadn't called. I'd been preparing for his call all week, for the follow-up call, for the call that would give me a chance to say all the things I hadn't been able to say during the initial call because I'd been so stunned. I was going to tell him that he was a schmuck and an asshole and a fuckhead and an idiot, and I didn't know what I'd ever seen in him in the first place. I was going to say that he and Kate Pearce deserved each other. I was going to warn him that she was going to leave him again, just like she had the first time, and he'd better not come crawling back to me, because I won't take him back, not in a million years, not for all the tea in China, not if he was the last man on Earth. I was going over this stuff again in my head while I was sitting at my desk late on Friday when it hit me: maybe Tom wasn't going to call me, ever. Maybe he thought "I'm in love with somebody else" covered everything. Maybe he wasn't even going to give me the satisfaction of telling him what a schmuck and an asshole and a fuckhead and an idiot he was. That would be just like him, the bastard.

Suddenly I knew what I had to do. I had to call him. I had to call him and tell him that we needed to have a talk, a face-to-face talk, that I deserved at least that much consideration. If nothing else, we had the business of cohabitation to discuss. I mean, was he planning to pay his half of the rent for the next month? Did he expect me to warehouse his personal effects indefinitely? Tom might be hoping to swoon around in a sex haze a while longer, content to wear his friends' old suits to work so he could put off a confrontation with me, but I had details to attend to, plans to make.

I looked at my watch. It was six-fifteen. I realized I had to make the call right away, because if I didn't catch him before he left work, I'd be forced to wait until Monday, because I didn't know where he was sleeping. I knew who he was sleeping with, but I had no idea where. I grabbed my purse and headed for the stairwell, in search of a pay phone. I couldn't wait until Monday. If I waited until Monday, I'd explode.

"Hey there," Henry said. He was heading out the door.

"Hi, Henry," I said.

"Where are you off to?"

"Nowhere."

"You want to grab some dinner?"

"With you?" I said.

"That's what I was thinking."

I looked at my watch. Tom had probably left the office already, anyway. He was probably hurrying home to have sex with Kate. That's what you do in the beginning, you hurry home. The shithead.

"Fine," I said. "That would be fine with me."

So we went out to dinner. Henry and me. And I was so distracted by thoughts of Tom not calling and Tom fucking Kate and Tom in bed with Kate, spent, thinking idly about not calling me, that it wasn't until my second glass of wine that I looked across the table at Henry, really looked at him. He was telling me a story about his first apartment in New York. He's really good-looking, I thought. He was too good-looking, in fact. I've always thought that dating a really good-looking guy would be like buying a white couch: it might be nice to have, but you'd waste all that time *worrying* about it. (Tom isn't bad-looking, if you're wondering, but he isn't particularly good-looking either — Tom is the equivalent, I'd say, of a subtly patterned beige couch.)

Anyway: Henry. At some point, and I don't know exactly when it happened, the conversation turned, and Henry and I were no longer two coworkers talking about careers and apartments, but a man and a woman, slightly drunk, in a Chinese restaurant with a candle in the middle of the table. Actually, I do know when it happened. Henry had gotten up to go to the bathroom, and when he came back he had to kind of squeeze behind my chair to get back into his, and in the process of squeezing by he leaned down and said, "You smell good." That's it, just "You smell good," but all of a sudden we were laughing a little more conspiratorially and touching each other's forearms to punctuate our sentences and casually mentioning movies we'd like to see and then agreeing that we ought to go see them together.

"Won't that be a problem for, what's his name, the guy in your column?" Henry said.

"We broke up," I said.

"Ah."

"Yeah. Well," I said. "Yeah."

"What happened?"

And so I told Henry what had happened with Tom, but I left out the more humiliating details, and the truth is there wasn't much of a story left without the humiliating details. I said that Tom and I wanted different things, for example, but I didn't indicate that what I wanted was Tom and what Tom wanted was Kate Pearce. And while I didn't exactly lie, it's safe to say that by the time I was through, Henry was left with the impression that Tom and I had sat down together one day and decided that our relationship, while wonderful, had run its course; that we'd arrived at this decision in a supremely rational and healthy manner, without the aid of sex with third parties or marital ultimatums or anything like that; and that we'd both walked away with no hurt feelings, only a little bit of self-knowledge and a twinge of fond regret. Even worse, though, I managed to imply that all of this had happened quite some time ago, and that I'd had a chance to gain perspective and — I'm ashamed to admit it, but I actually used this word — *closure*.

"Have you ever noticed that the Chinese don't have a good dessert?" Henry said when the check finally came.

"What do you mean?"

"Think about how much more money people would spend in Chinese restaurants each year if they had a halfway-decent dessert. They should just adopt something. Just, pretend it's theirs and start serving it."

"Tiramisu," I said.

"Perfect. It even sounds Chinese."

"Pretty soon people would be saying, 'I'm in the mood for tiramisu, let's get Chinese.'"

"You know what?" Henry said.

"What?"

"I'm in the mood for tiramisu."

So we paid the check and we walked to an Italian restaurant a few blocks away and sat at the bar and shared a tiramisu and some sambuca, and Henry told me about growing up in Florida and I told him about growing up in Arizona, and what with all the alcohol it started to feel like we had a lot in common, citrus fruit playing a prominent role in both of our childhoods, the disorienting absence of seasons, the longing for a life with snow days and fireflies and art museums displaying more than just shards of Native American pottery. I could end up having sex here, I thought. This is how people do it. They go out, they get drunk, they talk, one of them says that the other one smells good, and then they go home and have sex. Of course, here we had the added complication that Henry was my boss, but that sort of thing has been known to happen. Maybe not to me, but it happens. Did I want to be the kind of girl who has undefined-yet-presumably-meaningless sex with her boss? Could I be that girl? Was it even possible? Could I be the kind of girl who has undefined-yet-presumably-meaningless sex with her boss and regrets it the next morning but still wouldn't do anything different if she had the chance to do it all over again? You have to understand that up until this point in my life, the part of my brain devoted to Sexual Regret was populated entirely with people I *didn't* go to bed with. If I'd broken down and had sex with Lance Bateman, for example, when I was seventeen and desperately wanted to, I'm convinced that my entire life would have turned out differently. I say this not because I'm under some sort of delusion about Lance's sexual prowess, but because sleeping with him would have gotten me over the hump, so to speak, and then I would have gone on through my life and slept with all the other people I regret not sleeping with, or most of them anyway, and I'd be a little harder now, and a little more damaged, and sort of a slut — but I'd be wiser, too. I'd be a wise slut.

I find I'm trying to explain how it is that Henry ended up back at my apartment.

I think one of the reasons I've had sex with so few people is because it took me so long to figure one simple thing out: men ask once. They don't even ask, really. They try. Men try once. That's why Holly Hunter was so upset when she got stuck at Albert Brooks's house and couldn't go have sex with William Hurt after he'd groped her left breast in front of the Jefferson Monument. She knew she might not get a second chance. And she was right — she didn't get a second chance, because the plot got in the way. A part of me knew that if I didn't go ahead and go home with Henry that first night, then it was never going to happen between us. The window of opportunity would close forever. And so, when Henry asked if he could come up and see my apartment after he walked me home, I said yes.

When we got inside, I went into the kitchen to get us some drinks. I could hear Henry poking around in the other room.

"Beer okay?" I called.

"Perfect," said Henry.

"Good."

"You play golf?" he said.

"No. Do you?"

"A little."

Henry materialized in the doorway to the kitchen. He leaned against the door frame with his arms folded across his chest and looked at me.

"You have a brother who plays golf who by chance stores his clubs in your entry hall?"

"No," I said.

"I'm starting to get the feeling that maybe I shouldn't be here."

"Why not?"

"He's been gone, what, a week?"

Was it that obvious?

"Longer than that," I said.

"No man who golfs often enough to keep his clubs in the entry-way would leave them for much more than a week."

"He hasn't been gone for very long, but it's been over for a while."

"Ah."

"You with your ahs."

"They give me time to think," Henry said.

"What are you thinking?"

"I'm just wondering when you're going to write about it."

"I don't know if I'm going to."

"It seems like just the sort of thing you write about."

"I'm going to write about the Chinese restaurants and the tiramisu."

"I think you're not going to write about it until you're sure it's over."

I didn't say anything.

"Which means you're not sure it's over," Henry said. "Which means I should probably go."

"I'm not sure that's absolutely necessary," I said, throatily. The second the words were out of my mouth, I regretted them. Maybe he was looking for a graceful way out, and I'd just made that impossible. Maybe I'd blocked his escape route. "If you want to leave, you should go," I said, and then, in a panic — fearing that he might now think I *wanted* him to leave — I amended it with this: "But don't not stay because of, you know, him."

Okay, people: this is what I'm talking about. If you don't have sex somewhere between the ages of, say, sixteen and twenty-two, it seems to me that you miss out on some very important things. There's a whole lot of crucial stuff I never learned, like, for example, how you get from a meaningful stare over the tiramisu into bed without completely humiliating yourself. Sometimes I think that there's a whole world of signs and signals and maybe even secret handshakes that I completely missed out on, and the rest of humanity is busy indicating to one another over water coolers and in supermarket checkout lines whether or not they want to have sex, and if they do, whether they're in it for just a good time or whether they think it might lead somewhere, and I'm just walking along, completely oblivious.

Henry, fortunately, saved me. He put his beer on the kitchen counter and took my face in his hands and gave me a kiss, quite a kiss if you must know, and then he said, "What do you want me to do?"

"I think you should stay," I said.

"Good."

"So."

"So."

We moved to the couch. Things progressed. When it became glaringly apparent where this all was headed, I felt something approaching panic. I did the only thing I could think of, which was excuse myself to go to the bathroom.

I shut the door and sat down on the toilet. I'm embarrassed to tell you what I was thinking — Okay, I'll tell you: "What if I cry afterwards," is what I was thinking. Then, even more alarming: "What if I cry *during*." And while I might be accused of over-thinking things, crying was a distinct possibility. Not only was I about to have sex with someone I wasn't in love with, I was about to have sex with someone I wasn't in love with while I was in love with somebody else. I'd never done anything remotely like that in the past, and for all I knew my central nervous system wouldn't be able to take it. Fuses would blow. Plus, I'd been doing a lot of crying in that bed in the past seven days, and it was quite conceivable that I'd developed some sort of Pavlovian response to the sheets. Perhaps we should do it on the floor, I thought. Yes, the floor. I felt better for a moment, until I realized that it was entirely possible that Henry was already in the bed — just how adult were we being here? — and if he was, there was no way I could get him out of it and onto the floor without appearing to be completely out of my mind. All of this made me think of the last time I'd had sex on the floor, with Tom, of course, many, many months before this, back in my old apartment. I remembered how I'd opened my eyes midway through and found myself staring at the underside of my kitchen table (yes, this was sex on the floor *in the kitchen*) and I'd noticed that somebody had stuck a wad of green chewing gum under it, and when I realized I was thinking about who put that gum there instead of about what was going on, sexually speaking, I'd gotten incredibly depressed. I told Bonnie about it the next day, and she assured me it was no big deal, that sometimes she found herself mentally packing her kids' lunch boxes while she was having sex with her husband Larry, which only served to depress me further. Now, of course, sitting in the bathroom all these months later, I realized that the reason Tom and I had been having sex on the kitchen floor in the first place was probably because Tom was trying to gauge the state of passion in our relationship, and I'd been lying there, thinking about gum. *She's like a drug.*

I stood up. I looked at my face in the mirror over the sink. It seemed clear to me that something was about to change, and I didn't know if it would be a good thing or a bad thing. I didn't know anything, really, except that I was going to go out there and have sex with Henry, and while it wasn't necessarily going to blot Tom from my mental landscape completely, it would probably make him recede a little into the distance, for a while anyway, and that was fine with me.

I opened the door to the bathroom. Henry had indeed made his way into the bedroom, and while he wasn't physically in the bed, he was close enough to it that the floor wasn't an option, which turned out to be fine. We kissed awhile, and then we did it, and then Henry fell asleep while I stared at the ceiling moonily for an hour and a half, and then I got up to go to the bathroom and when I came back Henry was awake and we did it again, and then I fell asleep too, happy.

(Okay, I *know* you want details. I *know* you want to hear about dimensions of penises and descriptions of orgasms and positions and maneuvers and blowjobs and all that, but here's the problem: my mother is still alive. And as much as I'd like to tell you all that, if I did, I'd have to kill her. And my poor fathers, both of them, I don't think they could take it either. I'd have to kill them too. And my Grandma Texas. And any children I ever get around to having, once they learned how to read, I'd be forced to put them out of their misery. Still, I realize you've come a long way with me here, and you deserve to know a few things. You deserve to know that Henry turned out to be what is commonly described as Good In Bed. You also deserve to know that I realized for the first time why that particular quality in a man is so prized among women, if you get my drift, and I think you do . . .)

Seven

MAYBE YOU THINK I JUMPED INTO BED WITH HENRY AWFULLY fast for a person who was supposed to be in love with somebody else, I don't know. I mean, I think I jumped into bed with him awfully fast myself, so I can just imagine what you must be thinking. I feel I should point out that the whole thing was completely out of character. It was so far out of character, come to think of it, that it's entirely possible it circled all the way around back to being in character again. One of the hardest things about having a religious background like mine is that it makes it exceedingly difficult to figure out which parts of you are actually you and which parts aren't. That's where my eleven years of thirteen-dollar-an-hour psychotherapy inevitably ran into a brick wall. Whenever I faced a moral dilemma, whichever therapist I happened to be seeing at the time would say, "Trust yourself." That was the mantra. *Trust* yourself. Trust your*self*. And

I'd sit there in one of the clinic's orange molded-plastic chairs and I'd try to get into it, really I would, but I'd always come back to the fact that the one thing I'd learned in church was that I was not to be trusted.

I don't like to be in the business of blaming the church for things that have gone wrong in my life. I realize it might seem like I do an awful lot of it for someone who doesn't like to do it, but my feeling is that the rest of the world is happy bashing evangelical Christians and there is no need for me to pile on. I mean, surely a little low-grade looniness about sex is a small price to pay to go through life with the unshakeable conviction that you're going to end up in heaven. But the problem with growing up with a highly polarized, dualistic view of the world is that, if you ever decide to go off and do things your own way, all you get left with are the bad parts. The first thing I thought the night of the dinner party was not, as I believe I told you earlier, that the thing with the ring was probably a mistake. That was the second thing I thought. The first thing I thought was, *So this is how God has decided to punish me.* It was as if God had taken time out of his busy schedule of rescuing flood victims from rooftops and healing holes in newborn babies' hearts and decided to punish me by having Tom go out for the mustard and not come back. And I realize that I sound very matter-of-fact, very literal, about a thing that, if it exists at all, exists as a metaphysical reality, but that's another thing about evangelicals. We're very literal. Just try to suggest to an evangelical that sometimes a symbol is just a symbol and you'll see what I mean.

Gil-the-homosexual was an evangelical Christian when I met

him — now that he's gay, I'm not sure what he is. Gil was so
Christian back then that we met in a church basement, tutoring
underprivileged children. Our church ran an outreach program
in which a bunch of kids from the projects were bused in every
Tuesday night for us to influence. We sang Jesus songs at them
while they threw things at one another, and then we helped
them with their homework. The trick was to get assigned one of
the sweet seven-year-olds who you could surprise with gifts like
coloring books and sticker packs and pencil sets instead of a bel-
ligerent fourteen-year-old who greeted you each week with
"Whadja bring me?" Why we all did this week in and week out,
I don't know. The kids, I suppose, wanted the sticker packs. I
wanted a boyfriend. I wanted a boyfriend who was a Christian
but who wasn't uptight about it, who was good-looking and intelligent and had an interesting job and a sense of humor, who
said "fuck" when the situation warranted it, who had attempted
but been unable to finish St. Augustine's *City of God,* who could
argue politics with my mother and talk business with my father,
who liked Indian food and had nice friends and knew how to
dress and would like someday to live abroad. I took a look
around the church basement, and there was Gil.

I just realized that I haven't told you Gil's last name, which
means I've left out a big chunk of the Gil story. Gil's last name
was Chang. Gil Chang was not, however, Asian — which brings
me to the part of the Gil story I haven't gotten around to telling
you. Gil had gone to a tiny Baptist college down in Alabama
where, among other anachronisms, the students weren't allowed
to kiss each other until they'd gotten engaged. Well, everyone

got engaged. Everyone got engaged and then most of them got married and then a full sixty percent of them got divorced within three years of graduation. Anyhow, to hear him tell it, Gil had wanted to kiss a sweet girl in his New Testament class and the next thing you know he was married to her. Her name was Lily Chang, and she was Chinese, and Gil had figured it would be easier for their kids to go through life with an ethnically appropriate last name, so he'd taken Lily's, which was remarkably progressive of him, when you think about it. Lily turned out to be progressive, too, in her own way; eight months after they got married, she left him for an Argentinean tango instructor. Gil kept the friends and the furniture and the wedding presents and — in a truly bizarre move for which I never did receive a satisfactory explanation — Lily's last name.

That was one of the things I clung to when faced with evidence of Gil's latent homosexuality: the fact that he'd been married once already. *Gay men don't get married,* I'd think, whenever he'd say "righty-tighty, lefty-loosy" while trying to unscrew a lightbulb. Then, about the time that delusion started to wear thin, Gil and I started having sex. *Gay men don't have sex with women,* I'd think, every time he got up out of bed in the middle of the night to do his dusting. I had somehow gotten the idea that they couldn't do it, biologically speaking — that the hydraulics just wouldn't work. And the fact that Gil had been married before did explain a lot about him. That's why he had the queen-size cherrywood sleigh bed, in fact — Lily's parents had given it to them as a wedding present. It took up half of his apartment. The other half was filled with silver platters and brass candlesticks and crystal vases, and there were fourteen place settings of china lovingly displayed in a glass hutch in the living room, and matching coasters on every piece of furniture, all of which was polished to a high sheen.

I should have known about Gil, of course. I should have known the way you know about a dented can. But this is the thing: everyone has been warned about dented cans, but surely not every dented can is bad, or they wouldn't be allowed to sell them, right? *Someone's* buying those dented cans. *Someone's* taking them home and opening them up and examining the contents and then making a bet about whether or not the stuff inside is safe to eat. And let me tell you, when you're twenty-five, and a virgin, and you refuse to date anybody but a Christian — and not just any Christian but a *certain kind* of Christian — your options are all dented cans. When Gil and I finally broke up, I took another look around the church basement, and I had the closest thing I've ever had to an actual vision. There sat Brian Berryman. Single. Thirty-two. An attorney. Crown prince of the church basement. So morally upright he didn't believe in dating; he believed in praying. He'd been praying for a wife since he was sixteen. He'd drawn up a list of all the qualities he wanted her to possess, a list which he was continually revising, and then praying about, and then revising some more, and then informally circulating among the single women at the church. A woman of pure heart, the list would go. A gentle and quiet spirit. A submissive nature. *Is this what you want in a husband?* I heard a voice saying. Well, not an actual voice, but it was as clear as day. I realized that if I kept searching for hus-

bands in church basements I was going to end up with a seriously dented can. And Gil, for all his faults, had at least relieved
me of my virginity, which meant that it was now safe for me to
venture out into the world and date normal men who would
want to — who would *expect* to — sleep with me.

I ask you, what would you have done if you were me? What
would you have done? It's impossible to convey just what I was
up against. Years and years of appalling platitudes that were
preached at me as if they were gospel. *No one wants the second-
hand garments that have been pawed over on the sale table. No one
wants the flower that has been plucked before it has a chance to
bloom.* And for a long time this made perfect sense to me. Of
course no one would want a pawed-over garment. Of course no
one would want a flower that had already been plucked. And
then one day it hit me: *but I am not a* flower, *nor am I* clothing. I
was not an object. It felt really good to finally see through all of
that, and to this day I consider that revelation the beginning of
my admittedly somewhat stunted feminist awakening. Tom always said that I was traditional when being traditional suited
my purposes and liberated when being liberated did, and while
he did not intend this as a compliment, I always took it as one.
Still, I've often wondered why I've never been able to become a
full-blown feminist. Sometimes I think it's because, having left
one brand of self-righteous orthodoxy, I haven't wanted to
throw my lot in with another, but it's entirely possible that I'm
just too much of a fucking ninny. Oh well. I am feminist enough
to be angry about a few things. I mean, it's one thing to live in a
society that views women as objects, and quite another to go to

church as a young girl and have it pounded into your head to look at yourself as one. It made me want to get pawed over just to spite them. So I did, and it was fun, and for a while there I thought I was free of all that. But I wasn't free of it, not really, not in a way that really counted. Because every time I stopped to think about what happened between Tom and me, a part of me couldn't help believing that the real problem was simply that Tom had lost interest in the gum he had already chewed. He'd been getting the milk for free, and therefore had not bought the cow, and now he was in the mood for a new cow. What right had I to be surprised? This was, after all, what I'd been warned about my entire life. I'd been told in no uncertain terms just what the fruits of sexual freedom would be — that I'd end up alone and unloved, unmarried and childless, an object of scorn and pity, without even the solace of my faith. And, well, lying in my bed the morning after I'd had sex with Henry, alone (because he'd left), unloved (I think it's safe to say I felt unloved), I was forced to ask myself — just what part of that wasn't turning out to be true?

I see that in trying to address the topic of my faith I have focused almost exclusively on sex. Surely there is more to the spiritual tradition of St. Paul and Thomas Aquinas and Martin Luther than that, is probably what you are thinking. There is. I will not bore you with any of it here, however. The truth is, I have complicated feelings about the whole thing. Certainly many of them are negative, and the ones that aren't negative are hard to put into words. And I suppose if I had been raised as a Christian Scientist, all of this craziness would revolve around something completely different, like going to the doctor. The way it would work would be like this: I wouldn't go to the doctor for a very long time, and when I finally did go, it would be a result of doubt and curiosity and a desperate need for medical attention, and when the world didn't stop turning because of my trip to the doctor it would create even more doubt, and pretty soon I'd be going to the doctor all the time and I wouldn't be a Christian Scientist anymore. Of course, I can see the ridiculousness of that. It's not always easy to see your own ridiculousness, though.

Eight

WHEN I WOKE UP THAT SATURDAY MORNING, HENRY HAD already left. I lay in bed by myself for a while, trying to feel my feelings. That was one of the things I had worked on in therapy. The problem with feeling my feelings lately was that whenever I actually sat down and tried to feel them, I felt like throwing up. I tried to remember what Janis Finkle had said to me. *Let them pass through you like a wave. Watch them the way you watch clouds floating by.*

I sat up. I'm not going to be a lunatic about this, I decided. It was casual sex. I'm going to be casual about it. I got out of bed and headed for the bathroom, which is where I found the note. It was propped up against the mirror over the sink. I immediately picked up the phone and called Cordelia. (Cordelia is my friend for situations like this, not Bonnie.)

"What did it say?" Cordelia said when I got to the part about the note.

"Keep in mind that he's my boss," I said. "So I think it's meant as some kind of office joke."

"What did it say?" she asked again.

"Fine work."

"Fine *work*?"

"Yeah," I said. "It said, 'Alison. Fine work. Henry.'"

"Okay, I can see how he meant that to be funny," Cordelia said. "Witty. Something other than offensive."

"Me too."

"Still."

"I know."

"But you shouldn't worry."

I was worried. "It seems to me, if you have amazing sex with a person, and not just once but twice, you stick around for the morning part, right?" I said. "That just seems logical to me."

"You did it twice?" she said.

"Yes."

"Twice, one right after the other, or twice, two separate times?"

"Two separate times," I said. "He fell asleep in between. Does that matter?"

"Not really," said Cordelia. "I just like to have all the infor-mation."

"What do you think?"

"Okay," Cordelia said. She took a breath. "It's possible that you were having amazing sex and he was just, you know . . . having sex."

I didn't say anything for a moment. "That happens?"

"The whole time I was with Jonathan, I was having the time of my life," Cordelia said. "He was just lying there, wishing I was an underwear model."

"He told you that?"

"We had a very honest relationship," Cordelia said. "The fuckhead."

Jonathan really was a fuckhead, and he did some truly horrible things to Cordelia, and she always says that she stayed with him for so long because of the sex. Sex is very important to Cordelia. She's had a lot of it, and she has a number of interesting theories about it. In fact, the real reason I knew I wasn't having great sex with Tom before I finally had great sex with Henry was because of one of Cordelia's theories. Here's the theory. Really great sex is like movie sex. If you watch people having sex in movies and you say to yourself, *"Oh, nobody has sex like that except in movies,"* then you should know that you're not having great sex. I tried to call Cordelia on this once, back when I first started sleeping with Gil-the-homosexual. "What about *Fatal Attraction*?" I remember saying to her. "With the water running? And the dishes in the sink?" Cordelia just raised one of her eyebrows in the way that she does, and I knew that if Cordelia felt that way there had to be something to it.

"Okay, I've just had this amazing time," I said. "Twice. I've had two amazing times. And I'm lying there, staring up at the ceiling, and do you know what I'm thinking?"

"What are you thinking?"

"How long before we reach the point in our relationship where I can go into the bathroom afterwards and put on my moisturizer."

"You're sick," Cordelia said. "You do realize that."

"I do."

"This guy is not that guy," Cordelia said. "Trust me."

"I know."

"It would take *a lot* to turn this guy into that guy," she said. "But maybe he can be your greasy pancake," she said.

"My what?" I said.

"When you're making pancakes, the first one soaks up all the grease on the griddle, so you have to throw it away," said Cordelia. "Henry can soak up all the grease left over from Tom. Then your griddle will be ready to go."

"I don't think that's a very good metaphor," I said, "but I like it."

"It's my mom's," she said. "Only she *married* her greasy pancake. 'Don't make the same mistake I made,' she says whenever they have a fight. 'Throw away your greasy pancakes.'"

"So what am I supposed to do?" I said.

"That's easy," said Cordelia. "Enjoy your greasy pancake. And then throw him away."

I'm worried that I've given you the impression that I was upset about what had happened with Henry, and I should probably take a moment here to correct that impression. I was not really all that upset. I mean, I knew that on a purely objective level I should be offended — Henry slinking off in the middle of the night, the "fine work" note, the fact that he did not call me later that Saturday or even on Sunday — but I also must admit that I felt a certain undeniable thrill. I mean, the man didn't even know my middle name! It was like I was suddenly living a life I'd only read about in books, like I woke up one day and was suddenly a rodeo cowboy or a sixteenth-century Portuguese explorer or a geisha girl. That's how big it felt. Having lived my life with a certain set of restrictions and expectations and admonitions — most of which boil down to the idea that sex is to be used to extort a lifelong commitment from a man, and anything less than that is considered a tactical failure on the part of the woman, with the direst of consequences — there I was, finally throwing caution to the wind after years and years of almost throwing it. And say what you will about the perils of sexual freedom, nobody had ever told me the whole truth, which is that it feels an awful lot like actual freedom.

On Sunday afternoon I wrote a column about the Chinese restaurants and the tiramisu. I realize this isn't much of a transition, but that's the problem with trying to tell a story like this: you need too many transitions. I'm used to writing columns, very short columns, and as a result I'm not very good at transitions. A good column explores one idea, boom, you're in and then you're out, and then the reader makes his own transition, to another article or tying his shoelaces or getting off the bus or whatever. But I have to keep everything moving forward here, and all you need to know about the rest of that particular weekend is that I wrote my column on Sunday afternoon, the way I always do, and on Monday morning I walked to the office, the way I always do, with my column about the Chinese restaurants and the tiramisu on a computer disk. I looked good. I mean, I looked better than I usually do, although I didn't realize how much better until I got to the office and Olivia and Matt couldn't stop commenting on it. I suppose I looked the way a girl who'd slept with her boss on Friday night would look on Monday morning, but I didn't want Olivia to figure that out, which is why I ended up telling the two of them about Tom. Olivia can smell these things a mile away. She's a big believer in the "where there's smoke, there's fire" school of human sexuality — namely, if you think two people might be sleeping together, they are (with the corollary that if you think a person might be gay, he is).

"Why are you all dressed up?" said Matt.

"I'm not," I said.

"Yes you are. Olivia," Matt said, "don't you think Alison looks exceptionally good this morning?"

Olivia looked me up and down slowly and nodded her head.

"Tom and I broke up," I said.

"What?" Olivia said. "When did this happen?"

"I don't want to talk about it," I said. "You just wanted to know why I look good, and now you know."

"Because you're back on the prowl," said Matt.

"I'm not on the prowl," I said. "I just felt bad, so I figured I should try to look as good as possible so I wouldn't end up seeing myself in a mirror and feeling even worse."

"What happened?" said Olivia.

"I don't want to talk about it," I said.

"Of course you want to talk about it," said Olivia. "Tell us what happened."

I looked at the two of them. It was clear I wasn't going to get away with not talking about it. "He thinks we're growing apart."

"Bullshit," said Olivia.

"Why is that necessarily bullshit?" Matt said to Olivia. "Maybe they were growing apart."

"That's just the kind of bullshit excuse men always come up with," Olivia said. "It means he wants to fuck strangers, that's what it means."

"Actually, I'm pretty sure he knows who he wants to fuck," I said.

"Who?" said Olivia.

"Her name is Kate Pearce," I said. "And he's already fucking her."

"How do you know that?" said Olivia.

"It's been going on since May," I said.

"He told you that?" said Olivia.

"He said he was in love with somebody else. I figured out the rest."

Olivia walked over and sat one of her haunches on my desk. "Who is she?" said Olivia.

I told them a little about Kate. I said she was bony, and her hair stuck to her head like a helmet. I said she had a little-girl frailty that made me want to puke. I told them she had given Tom a lasagna for his birthday, and I should have known then where this all was headed, but I didn't. (I'm tempted to leave the lasagna out of this, because it's kind of a confusing detail, as details go — Kate Pearce is not the lasagna-making type — but Kate did in fact make a lasagna for Tom, early on, before the sex part of their affair started, and I'll tell you something: it was a very crafty move.)

"What do you mean, bony?" Matt said. "You mean thin?"

"She means bony," Olivia said. "There is still such a thing as bony."

"No. He's right. She's thin," I said. "She's beautiful. She's thin and beautiful."

"She's *new*," said Olivia.

"That's the thing. She's not new," I said. "They went out for three years in college, and then she dumped him." Then I told Matt and Olivia my theory, which I had spent the greater part of the past week developing. When Tom was two years old, his mother ran off to Hollywood to become a movie star, although the closest she got was a small recurring role as a nurse on a show called *Daniel Denby, Medical Doctor.* Tom's grandmother, who ended up raising him, would put him in his pajamas and sit him down in front of the television set every Thursday night to see if he could catch a glimpse of his mother, although even that often ended in disappointment, because her part was so small and she got cut out of episodes at random. All of which, it seemed to me, explained a few things about Tom's psychology. He had a certain amount of anger towards women. He had a pronounced unconscious longing for the lost mother. And my theory was that Kate's reentry into Tom's life after all these years had triggered those feelings and he was powerless to resist them.

"Yes," said Olivia. "He's reenacting his childhood psycho-drama."

Matt turned to me and said, "And guess who's Grandma."

I slumped my head down on my desk.

Olivia started to pace around the office. "It's perfect. He wants the woman who abandoned him. He can't help it. It's hardwired into him. His seeming inability to commit to Grandma —"

"Please," I said.

"This time, though, Mommy wants him too. They start having that incredibly hot sex that you can only have when it's really about something else, something primal, something transgressive, only Tom doesn't know that is what's going on. He just thinks he's found his soul mate. He thinks he's found his missing piece."

"I feel sick," I said.

Olivia looked at me. "Then again, I could be wrong," she said.

"I'm going to kill myself," I said.

"God knows I've been wrong before," said Olivia.

"Guys want to have sex with their old girlfriends. End of story," Matt said. Then he turned to Olivia. "And I can't believe you get paid to write an advice column."

Olivia left to get a cup of coffee, and after a bit Matt came over and sat on the edge of my desk.

"You realize you're much better off this way," Matt said.

"What do you mean?" I said.

"When somebody leaves you, it's always better if they leave you to be with somebody else," said Matt.

"Why is that?" I said.

"Because otherwise it means they just really, really can't stand you."

I just looked at him.

"It's much less personal this way," said Matt.

"It feels pretty personal," I said.

"Trust me," he said.

"I'll try," I said.

Nine

I MET BOB, MY BLIND DATE, AT AN ITALIAN RESTAURANT ON Tuesday night after work. I walked in and spotted him instantly. He was the bald guy sitting at the bar. He paid for his drink, and then we sat down at a table.

"How old are you?" said Bob. "Do you mind if I ask?"

"Thirty-two," I said. "And no, I don't mind. How old are you?"

"Forty-six," he said.

"You're forty-six?" I said.

"Yes," said Bob.

"Oh," I said.

"What?"

"Nothing," I said. "I'm just surprised Bonnie didn't mention our age difference."

"I don't consider this an age difference," said Bob.

"You don't consider fourteen years an age difference?" I said.

"Not really, no," he said.

"When was the last time you dated a sixty-year-old?" I said.

Bob leaned back in his chair and looked at me through half-closed eyes in a way that I'm sure he believed was incredibly seductive. "Larry told me you might be trouble."

"What did he say?"

"I don't remember exactly. I just got the impression that you might be trouble," said Bob. "Does my age bother you?"

"Kind of, yes," I said.

"How come?"

"Because, someday, when I'm forty, maybe I'll want to go out with a guy who's forty-six and single and a doctor and I won't be able to because you'll all be out on dates with thirty-two-year-olds with fresher eggs."

"Physiologically speaking, a thirty-two-year-old's eggs aren't really that fresh," said Bob. He got all medically, in that way that doctors sometimes get. "The idea of thirty-five being the cutoff is sort of a myth. Fertility itself dramatically decreases from thirty-five on, but you start seeing statistically significant increases in chromosomal irregularities much earlier."

"How much earlier?" I said.

"Twenty-eight, twenty-nine. If I were a woman, I would've had all my kids by thirty. It's not a popular position these days, of course, but it's scientifically sound."

There was a long pause.

"You cannot have this conversation with women on dates," I finally said.

"And why is that?" said Bob.

"Because," I said. "Because I forbid it."

He laughed. "You forbid it."

"Yes," I said. "As a human being who is forced to share this planet with you, I forbid you from ever having this conversation with another woman with whom you are on a date."

"I wouldn't have this conversation with you if you were any older. Trust me. I get fixed up with a lot of thirty-five-year-olds and I never even mention it," said Bob. "I mean, a single thirty-five-year-old woman takes one look at me and thinks, here's my chance to get a baby in under the wire and dramatically decrease my chance of getting breast cancer."

Maybe I should throw something at him, I thought. One of these crusty dinner rolls. Just pelt him with it.

"I just read an interesting article," he said. "It claimed that women who are in their forties who are having trouble getting pregnant shouldn't worry, because the technology is evolving so fast, they can just wait another twenty years and have a baby in their sixties."

That's it, I thought. I picked up my dinner roll and threw it at him. It glanced off his right temple and then hit the floor and rolled a few feet before coming to rest underneath a neighboring table. Bob shut up for a second, and then he started to laugh. He was a much better sport about it than I would have expected, actually. He laughed and laughed, like getting hit in the head with a piece of bread was the funniest thing that had ever happened to him.

"See, that's great. That's great. Most girls wouldn't do that. Throw food at a blind date."

"It was a first for me," I said.

"Anyway," said Bob. "You don't have anything to worry about. You won't still be dating when you're forty."

"How do you know that?" I said.

"Because I know," said Bob. "I know what's out there."

There were many things that were bothering me about this date, and I found myself, as I sat there, listening to Bob tell me what exactly it was that was wrong with the women who were still "out there," trying to distill it down to its essence. I finally put my finger on it. Bob thought he was the prize. It didn't matter that he was fourteen years my senior. It didn't matter that he was dull, or that he had no hair to speak of, or even that the tip of his nose moved ever so slightly whenever his upper lip touched his lower one. Still, somehow, Bob got to be the prize. And I don't mean to make it sound like I had nothing to do with it — I found myself thinking he was the prize too! I didn't even *like* him, and still I considered him the prize. And lest you think it was because he was a doctor, let me say that I associate the desire to marry a doctor with a particular order of bourgeois thinking I have somehow miraculously been spared, so it wasn't that. It was worse than that. It was that he was a chair. Life was a game of musical chairs, and it was somehow clear to both Bob and me that when the music stopped, somebody would be sitting on him and I just might be left standing.

I spent the rest of the evening playing with this idea, rolling it around in my mind, trying to see it from every angle, and as I did, it slowly revealed itself to me to be what it actually was, which was utterly ridiculous. If one of us is a chair on this date, I finally decided, it's me. *I'm* the chair. It felt good, getting to be the chair. Now that I stop to think about it, I wonder if this is the way a certain type of man feels whenever he goes out with a woman who falls shy of Christy Turlington in the looks department. I have no idea how things work if one of the people on a date looks like Christy Turlington — surely a different set of rules applies — but if there is anything that interests me less than the problems of unbelievably beautiful women, it is the problems of men who want to date unbelievably beautiful women. Anyhow, I sat through the remainder of my dinner with Bob awash in a sense of my own chairness, which at the time felt dangerously close to healthy self-esteem, although I see now that it wasn't. I see now that the fact that I'd managed to flip the whole thing over on its head didn't mean anything more than that: I'd managed to flip the whole thing over on its head. Still, it felt good at the time and I'd be lying if I said it didn't.

I was so preoccupied, really, thinking things silently to myself that it wasn't until midway through dessert that I realized I'd made my way through this date being completely and uncharacteristically low-key. I was so low-key I hardly recognized myself. I didn't even have that feeling I always have on blind dates — I'd only been on two blind dates in my life, but I recall quite plainly having this particular feeling while on both of them — where you try to make the other person fall for you simply so whoever did the fixing up will be convinced that you're desirable. Fuck that, I remember thinking as I looked across the table at Bob, who was droning on about his time-share in Maui, the tip of his nose dipping every time he encountered a word containing a B, an M, or a P. I'm desirable. *I'm the chair!*

Bob, for his part, didn't seem to notice that I wasn't saying much. He paid the check, and we walked up Walnut Street towards my apartment. When we got to Rittenhouse Square, we walked across it, towards the fountain, which was lit up and running. It was really quite beautiful.

"Do you believe in love?" Bob said to me when we reached the fountain.

"Excuse me?"

"Do you believe in love?" said Bob.

"Of course I do."

"No. Really think about it."

"Everybody believes in love," I said.

"Everybody thinks that they believe in love," said Bob. "But if everybody actually did, things would be much different."

I started to worry where all this was headed. I once went on a terrifically bad first date with a guy who, when I told him I was ready to go home, reached across the table and took one of my hands in his and said, "If we're going to have problems, let's just have them." Perhaps my new understated charm was more powerful than I thought.

"I feel like I should tell you that I'm not going to call you," Bob said when we got to my front door.

Or perhaps not.

"I'm at a point in my life where I like to be honest with the women that I go out with. It's a thing with me."

"That's very considerate of you," I said.

"Thank you," Bob said. "That's why I do it."

I opened the front door and stepped inside. Then I turned and looked at him.

"I feel like I should tell you that if you had called me, I would have waited two weeks to call you back, and then done so only at a time when I was certain you'd be at work, at which point I'd have said something vague and unconvincing into your machine about how busy I was, and how I'd give you a call when I came up for air. And then I never would have," I said. "Come up for air, I mean."

I smiled sweetly and shut the door in his face.

Ten minutes later my phone rang.

"How was your date?"

It was Henry.

"Words cannot describe it," I said.

"Give me the high point and the low point."

"Well," I said. "I had to throw a dinner roll at his head to make him shut up."

He laughed. "And the high point?"

"There was no high point," I said.

"Come on. There had to be something."

This moment is the high point.

"My salmon wasn't bad," I said.

"At least you got a nice piece of fish out of it," said Henry. "Can I stop by?"

"Now?" I looked at the clock in the kitchen. It was past eleven.

"I'm in your neighborhood," Henry said. "I'm at a pay phone. I'm standing next to a gigantic garbage can with a padlock on it. So the garbage can*not* escape."

"I don't know," I said.

"How about this. I'm going to pretend that I got cut off, and then I'll show up on your doorstep, at which point you can do with me what you will."

The phone clicked off, and I did a little dance.

I felt so close to Henry after we had sex that night that we ended up having one of those conversations where you feel like there is no use hiding anything anymore, you've just given yourself so entirely to the other person that you feel like running around your apartment and opening up your drawers and closets and cabinets and pulling out all sorts of shameful things and arraying them on the bedspread and shouting, "Look at this! And this! But love me!"

"Promise you won't laugh," I said.

"I promise," Henry said.

"Three."

He started to laugh.

"I'm sorry, it's just, three," said Henry. He cocked his head up on his palm and looked at me with almost scientific interest. "How old are you?"

"Thirty-two," I said.

"That's one a decade," said Henry.

"I wasn't having sex when I was ten."

"Apparently not."

"So, does that pose some sort of problem for you?" I said.

"I don't think so. It's kind of sweet," he said. "I suddenly feel this strange compulsion to kiss you on your forehead."

He leaned over and kissed my forehead.

"Tell me about them," he said.

"Who?"

"The Big Three."

I just looked at him.

"Wait," said Henry. "*I'm* number three?"

"Didn't I just tell you that?"

"I thought I was number four," Henry said. "I thought you meant three besides me."

"You're number three."

"Oh, God, that's, that's . . . tragic. Tragic is what that is. That is a tragedy. You are a one-woman humanitarian crisis."

"I shouldn't have told you."

"No. You were right to tell me. I just feel like I should have done better work here. Given you my A material."

"That wasn't your A material?"

"I don't know what that was," Henry said. "That was my slightly drunk, ringing-from-a-pay-phone material. You deserve better."

"Next time," I said.

Henry rolled over and sat up. "It's perfectly clear you can never sleep with me again. This sort of exclusivity will get you nowhere. You should get on the phone the minute I walk out the door. You could get those numbers up into the respectable range in no time."

"How many would be respectable?" I said. "These days, I mean. For a woman my age."

"Nine," said Henry.

"Nine?"

"Every woman I sleep with, I seem to be about number nine," said Henry.

"Really?"

"Come to think of it, I'm *always* number nine," he said. "Those sluts have been lying to me."

Henry got out of bed and headed for the bathroom.

"Don't ask me how many people I've slept with, because I'll be forced to lie to you," he called from the bathroom. "We're operating with an unprecedented amount of honesty here, and I'd like to maintain that as long as possible."

"Okay," I said.

"Good."

"Three," I could hear Henry saying. "Jesus Christ."

Ten

EARLY THE NEXT MORNING, MY PHONE RANG.

It was Bonnie.

"You're sure in a good mood," said Bonnie.

"Yes, I am," I said.

"So it went well?"

"It was unbelievable."

"Honey," Bonnie called to Larry. "Alison liked Bob."

"No. Actually — shit."

"What?"

"I didn't like Bob. Or he didn't like me," I said. "It didn't go well."

"Then what are you talking about?"

Sleeping with Henry is not normally the sort of thing I would tell Bonnie, at least not right away, for reasons which the upcoming conversation will make glaringly apparent. But I was trapped, and so I told her.

"He just rang your doorbell and you had sex with him?" said Bonnie, her voice trilling up an octave as she hit the last three words.

"No," I said. "He called me from a pay phone first. He only wanted to talk to me, anyway. The sex part just happened."

"Alison, you can't let your boss call you up from a pay phone in the middle of the night and come by and have sex with you."

"It wasn't like that," I said, although I realized as I said it that it was exactly like that.

"It's just not smart," she said.

"Well, maybe I'm tired of being smart."

Bonnie didn't say anything.

"Maybe that's my problem," I said. "Thinking five moves ahead all the time."

"I'm not saying you should think five moves ahead. But how about one move. The move where he stops sleeping with you and he's still your boss."

"Maybe I don't want to think at all. Maybe I'm just going to let things happen for once in my life."

"Alison, I know you're upset about Tom. It's okay to be upset about it. The rest of this isn't you. Maybe you should work on being alone for a while."

"I am alone, Bonnie."

"I mean alone in the way that you're by yourself and you're not having sex with anybody else."

I could hear Larry say to Bonnie, "Alison had sex with Bob? Go, Alison."

"Tell him I didn't," I said to Bonnie.

"She didn't have sex with Bob. She had sex with her boss."

"Still," Larry said. "Go, Alison."

"Why can't you be like that?" I said to Bonnie. "I think this is a good thing for me."

"I can't help it. I'm just worried about you," she said.

"What are you worried about, exactly?"

"I'm worried that this guy could just be using you for sex, and when it's over you'll end up even more hurt than you already are," said Bonnie.

"Has it crossed your mind," I said, "that maybe I'm just using *him* for sex."

"Are you?" said Bonnie. She sounded intrigued.

"I'm not sure," I said. "But I'll tell you one thing. If I were going to use somebody for sex, I'd use him."

Later that day, I met Cordelia for lunch. She told me about her new boyfriend, Naldo, who was a waiter at Bookbinders and grew up in Wisconsin.

"He has a very big penis, which is a problem," she said.

"His penis is so large it's actually a problem?" I said.

"It doesn't interfere with the act itself," she said. "It's just, I'm suspicious of men with big penises."

"How come?"

"I think it's hard for them to be faithful, because they keep wanting to show it to people."

I considered this for a moment. "It's like having a really great car that you can only drive on a closed track," I said.

"And men like other people to see their cars. That one fact explains the entire city of Los Angeles. So for a man to have a really big penis and settle down with just one woman goes completely against his nature. Doubly against it."

"Maybe we should look for men with such tiny penises that they're ashamed of them," I said.

"Even men with tiny penises aren't ashamed of them," said Cordelia. "God knows they should be, but they never are."

I love Cordelia. The two of us are alike in a lot of ways, but one of the truly oddest ways that we are alike is that she was brought up with the same degree of maniacal religious intensity as me, only she was raised as a Mormon, not a Christian. Cordelia's family is so Mormon that her great-great-grandfather actually shook hands with Brigham Young. That is, in fact, how her grandmother introduces herself when she meets other Mormons: "You're shaking the hand of someone who shook the hand of someone who shook the hand of Brigham Young." And while it might not seem obvious that that would make us have much in common, the truth is it's frightening the degree to which the two teams are reading from the same playbook. It was actually kind of upsetting when Cordelia and I finally sat down and compared notes. That bit I told you, about being told that no man would want a flower that was plucked before it had a chance to bloom? Well, this is how they did it in Cordelia's church. First, each teenage girl was handed a long-stemmed white rose. Then there'd be a little chastity lecture by one of the young married women in the church. (And it's always the women who do this sort of thing; people are shocked when they find out that the hand that wields the clitoridectomy scalpel belongs to a woman, but it doesn't surprise me one bit.) Then, the chastity lady would walk around the room and — *with a dirty hand* — scrunch up each girl's rose and pull off a clump of the petals and ask her if that's what she wanted to be, if that's how she wanted to end up, if that's what she wanted to present to her husband on her wedding night. Which could explain why Cordelia's rebellion has managed to outstrip even my own.

I would like to take a moment here to make a point about women and the church. Every so often, I will find myself in a conversation about what the church sees as the role of women, which is not high on my list of conversations I like to have, but when it comes up I try to deal with it. At some point, whoever I'm talking to (and again, it's always a woman who ends up saying this sort of thing, although I suppose if a man said something like this to me I would probably punch him) will try to explain why it is that she doesn't mind that in her tradition women are not allowed to preach, or to serve communion, or to teach men, or to be elders. Why she doesn't mind that her primary task is to have babies and submit to the leadership of her husband. Why she doesn't even see any of this as a *problem*. "One isn't worse than the other," these women always say; "the roles are just *different*." And what I say to them is this. I say, that is not true. One *is* worse than the other. It is worse to be the follower, the submitter, the perpetual number two. Not just *different* from being the leader, the boss, the God-ordained number one — actually worse. And I suppose that one of the best things to come out of my friendship with Cordelia was this: I saw that on this particular subject, the Mormons and the evangelicals got along perfectly. The language they used was not just similar, it was identical. The metaphors they employed were not just similar, they were identical. Never mind the truly monumental theological distinctions. Never mind that they thought we were going to hell and we thought they were going to hell. When it came to controlling their women, the two sides agreed just fine.

"I'm not sure if your big penis theory is correct," I said to Cordelia. "Tom has a reasonably sized penis. Nothing to write home about."

"'Dear Mom and Dad, I just met a man with a reasonably sized penis,'" Cordelia said. "You're right. Nobody would write that letter."

"Anyhow, Kate had already seen it back in college, so I don't know how their affair can be pinned on his desire to show it to her."

"Unless" — and here Cordelia got quite animated, the way she does when she's talking nonsense — "unless it *grew*."

I took a bite of my salad.

"So he needed to show it to her again," she said.

I gave her a look.

"I agree it's unlikely," she said.

"I don't think penises grow much late in life," I said.

"Which is a shame, really," Cordelia said. She looked across the table at me. "You realize you're probably never going to understand this."

"You mean Tom?"

She nodded her head yes.

"But I have to," I said. "I can't stand not understanding it."

"That's what I thought when my marriage fell apart. But at some point I had to accept that I was never going to understand it, it was never going to make sense to me, I couldn't blame myself and I couldn't even blame him."

"You blamed him for a while," I pointed out.

"I know. But the man was just such a crazy sex fiend I knew it wasn't fair to blame him for it. So I started blaming life instead. Now I'm working on a new approach."

"What's that?"

"Accept life as it is. No," Cordelia said. "Affirm life. As it is."

This reminded me of those self-help books that tell you to accept your body as it is, and how I find it absolutely impossible to do so, because accepting my body as it is means that I'll be stuck with it as it is, and that I can't accept. I said as much to Cordelia.

"Which is why I can't affirm life as it is," I said. "If I affirm life as it is, I'm going to be stuck with it the way it is."

"You *are* stuck with it the way it is," she said.

"I know," I said. "But I don't want to accept it."

Eleven

I HAVE A THEORY THAT MOST MEN TREAT THE WOMEN THEY'RE dating badly, for at least part of the time. With the good ones, this period of bad treatment is just a phase, a working out of their conflicting feelings about commitment and mortality, until they finally come to terms with the idea of having sex with the same woman over and over and over again for the rest of their lives and then dying. The bad ones, well — therein lies the problem. If the good ones treat you bad and the bad ones treat you bad, it makes it kind of hard to tell the difference, right? My friend Angie met a guy through the personals, and after they'd been dating for seven months and were (she thought) very much in love, she discovered he was periodically driving by his ex-girlfriend's house and leaving little love notes in her mailbox. Angie never would have found out about it if she hadn't gone to her cousin's baby shower and overheard some woman going on about her old boyfriend and the notes and how pathetic he was and what did she ever see in him in the first place. The pathetic guy's name was Julian, and the woman's name according to her place card was Gennifer with a G, and Angie thought, isn't that funny, *her* Julian used to date a Jennifer, and so she went home and asked how Jennifer spelled her name and Julian said "with a G" and Angie kicked him, twice, once in each shin. But — and here's the perplexing part — he confessed and apologized and stopped doing it and now Angie and Julian have been married for two years and they seem very happy. Okay, they seem reasonably happy. They seem happy the way most of my married friends seem happy: the women seem relieved, like giant sea turtles who have found a suitable beach for their eggs and managed to lumber past the high tide line without getting sucked back into the ocean, and the men, well — the men seem to have made their peace with the sheer *inevitability* of it all.

Two days after Henry and I had sex that second time, I walked into his office and shut the door.

"Hi," I said.

"What's up?" said Henry. He was searching through a pile of papers on his desk.

"I was wondering if we could talk about our relationship," I said.

(I know. I *know.* I have no excuse for myself. In fact, I'm desperately trying to come up with an excuse, some sort of reasonable explanation for the conversation I am about to recount, and the truth is I have none. This is the part of myself that I'll never

understand, that will never make sense to me, and that I'd like
to see led out behind the barn one night and shot.)

"Relationship?" Henry said, still busy with the papers. "What
relationship?"

"You know," I said. *"This."*

Henry looked up from his papers.

"What?" I said.

"I just, I guess I didn't know we were involved in a relationship," said Henry.

"Well, what would you call it?"

"I don't know. I hadn't thought about it. I didn't know it needed
a name."

"We've slept together four times," I said.

Henry furrowed his brow. "We've slept together two times."

"We've slept together a total of four times, but on two separate occasions," I said.

"I'm not an expert, but if we're talking about our *relationship*" — he leaned mightily on the word, like it was one I'd
invented solely for the purposes of this conversation — "I think
that counts as two."

"What's your point?"

"My point is this conversation seems a little premature."

"Fine. Okay. I have my answer," I said. I headed for the door.

"What answer is that?" said Henry.

"This is just a fuck. Which is perfectly fine. I just wanted to
know."

"I wouldn't call it that," Henry said.

"Then what would you call it?"

"It's, ah, let me think." He leaned way back in his chair and gazed off into space. "It's a bit of fun. That's somewhere between 'just a fuck' and 'a relationship.'"

"Okay," I said. I felt slightly better.

"Excellent. So. We all clear here?"

"I think so," I said.

"Good," he said, and went back to his papers.

I turned to go. This is what you get for sleeping with your boss, I thought. This is what happens when you let your new boss call you from a pay phone at eleven o'clock at night and come over and have sex with you two times, for a total of four times on two separate occasions. You wanted fun. You wanted amazing. You wanted to be like the girls on *Sex and the City,* and Henry had played his part, he had delivered the goods, and it wasn't fair to him to act like a lunatic after the fact. He did not sign on for it. The man did not sign on for it.

"Well, I don't . . . I'm not interested in a bit of fun," I said.

"You aren't," said Henry.

"No," I said.

"Are you asking me to marry you?" said Henry.

"No."

"Are you asking me to ask you to marry me?"

"No."

"Would you like to move in together?"

"No."

"So I don't see the problem," said Henry.

"There's no problem," I said.

There was a long pause.

"Alison," Henry said, kindly. "Just because I happened to be Number Three doesn't mean you have to be in love with me."

"I'm not *in love* with you," I said.

"I know that," Henry said. "But you'll feel better if you keep reminding yourself you're not."

Is it inevitable, I ask you, that a girl like me will end up thinking she's in love with every man she goes to bed with? Is it simply unavoidable? I guess what I'm asking is: did you see this coming? Because I didn't. I honestly didn't. I think I honestly thought that I could have meaningless sex with Henry, that he could be my greasy pancake, and that I could just go on about my life, clipping along, taking him or leaving him, without so much as a backwards glance. And is that even possible for me? I'm not asking if it's optimal or desirable or good — simply if it's possible. I wonder. I wonder if I had jumped into bed with somebody else, somebody who, say, didn't speak English, would that have made my experiment in meaningless sex meaningless enough to avoid this sort of complication?

(Mind you, I am not speaking for all women here. I never presume to be speaking for all women, but I feel I have to point out that on this subject that is particularly true. I know there are women out there who manage to participate in this sort of activity without getting tangled up in feelings, without thinking they're in love with a man just because he's seen them walk naked from the bed to the bathroom and then back again. I know for a fact that such women do exist. Cordelia is one of them. Cordelia has had sex with eighteen men, a figure which I acknowledge is not at all astonishing for a woman thirty-four years of age and yet truly astonishes me. *Eighteen* men. At last count! But my point is this: she didn't fall in love with all of them. She fell in love with some of them.)

If the falling in love part *is* inevitable — mind you, I have not landed on this conclusion definitively, on the grounds that I have not yet collected enough data (I'm not even sure how many data points would be sufficient, but I'm thinking I need more than three) — then what does that mean for the respective parties involved? When I said that Henry did not sign on for my lunacy — is that in fact true? What exactly was he signing on for, having sex with me, if it wasn't a relationship and it wasn't lunacy? I have to believe that, even before the Number Three conversation, it must have been fairly obvious to Henry what he was dealing with, and I can't help but wonder what in the world he was thinking. What was he thinking? A few years ago, my friend Eric told me that the summer he turned thirteen, he used to have eight or nine orgasms a day, most of them by pressing up against one of the water jets in his neighbor's pool. A small part of me didn't believe him, a small part of me thought, okay, he must have some sort of problem, and a very big part of me thought I'm never going swimming with Eric ever again. I mention that now because it stuck with me — you watch, it'll stick with you, too — but also because, well, maybe it's as simple as that. Maybe that's what Henry was thinking — meaning, maybe he wasn't thinking anything at all. Maybe what I ought to keep in mind when I find myself trying to find some sort of

logic and reas~~~~
Eric humping his ne~~~~en and sex are concerned is simply

And another thing. Abo~ool.

sible that by the time I've coll~ata collection process. It's possible
conclusion on the inevitability of a ~nough data to come to a
with every man she sleeps with, I will no lo~~~e me falling in love
and the question will be moot. The act of exper~~be a girl like me
will change the fundamental nature of the sampl~mentation itself
should just accept it, accept that I will end up in love w~h every
man I go to bed with and, while I'm at it, accept that by the time
I've slept with enough people for this to no longer be the case, I
will have become a different person altogether.

Twelve

ONE OF THE BENEFITS OF WRITING A NEWSPAPER COLUMN IN A town like Philadelphia is that one is occasionally called upon to perform the sort of ceremonial duty that, in a larger city, would be performed by somebody who was actually famous. Usually this involves judging something, and usually I say yes.

That Thursday night was one such occasion. I had been called upon to judge pie. It was a food thing, and there were all sorts of categories, and somehow I got pie. Which was fine. I like pie. And it worked out quite well, really, in that immediately after the "I'm not in love with you" conversation with Henry, I got to leave work and go evaluate fourteen different pies for things like flakiness of crust and tastiness of filling. It was a work-sanctioned binge. Afterwards, I went home to change, and at around eight, I headed back to Reading Terminal for the party where they would announce the winners.

The Reading Terminal Market is one of the things that everybody loves about Philadelphia, and they're right to love it. It's a farmers' market built inside an old railroad terminal, and it's filled with Amish women selling honey in jars with those little gingham jar bonnets on top and smiling men offering three-dollar shoe shines. There's a stall that sells nothing but used cookbooks, and one that sells nothing but powdered doughnuts, and one that sells nothing but handmade pretzels. It manages to do all of this without being precious, which is no small feat. Tom and I used to go there together every Saturday morning for brunch. We'd buy the *Philadelphia Inquirer* and the *New York Times* at the newsstand and eat at the Down-Home Diner and then, on the way out, I'd stop by the Salumeria and pick up an interesting cheese. You need things like that in a relationship. You need things that remind you that it's better to be a part of a couple than to be on your own, because the idea of going to Reading Terminal every Saturday by yourself and reading the paper by yourself and buying cheese to go home and eat by yourself is almost too horrible to bear. As I headed up Market Street that evening, I wondered if Tom had taken Kate there the past Saturday, and if he hadn't, just how long it would be before he did so. It would be naive to think that he wouldn't — Saturday morning at Reading Terminal is just too perfect, and just because he'd left me, there was no reason to think he wouldn't try to salvage what was one of the best things about our relationship. I wondered what would happen if I walked in one day and saw Tom and Kate sitting in a booth at the diner, passing sections of the *New York Times* back and forth over coffee. I wondered if I'd have the courage to walk up to them and say something biting. I wondered if I could think up something biting to say that wouldn't sound like I'd thought it up in advance. Probably not, I decided. Then I walked through the big swinging doors and into Reading Terminal and I stopped thinking about Tom. There, standing underneath a large potted palm, was my arch enemy, Mary Ellen.

I realize it's wrong to introduce an arch enemy at this point in the story. It violates all sorts of dramatic principles — not that this story has been adhering with any sort of strictness to dramatic principles, but I like to believe that, up until now at least, none have been thrown down on the floor and violated. Oh, well. I have an arch enemy and her name is Mary Ellen. The reason I haven't mentioned her before now is that she's the kind of arch enemy that I forget about for long stretches of time. I rarely see her, for one thing. I read her column every week, though, just to see if she's still taking shots at me. I have, as a point of honor, never mentioned her in print, not once. I've always dealt with our supposed rivalry by appearing to rise above it, by pretending publicly at least that she was no more trouble to me than something unpleasant I'd accidentally stepped in, which is why I wish I could skip over this part entirely. I'd love to, but I can't, simply because I can't leave out of this story what happened that night.

I realize that up until now you've been thinking that the *Philadelphia Times* was the most marginal newspaper in Philadelphia, and now you're going to find out that there was an even more marginal one. It was called *Hello, Philly!,* and it was given away for free, just like our paper, but the *Times* was distributed in those metal boxes on street corners, just like a real newspaper, while *Hello, Philly!* was hung on people's doorknobs, just like those Pennysaver shopping circulars. This seemed like a huge distinction to us at the time. I realize that it all sounds very small-time, and there is a war going on inside of me, one side of which wants to impress upon you that it was not small-time at all while the other wants to go ahead and give in. I give in. At any rate, like most small-time things, when one was in the middle of it, it felt relatively normal-sized.

When Mary Ellen got a job writing for the doorknob paper, she immediately caused the sort of sensation I have always been meaning to cause and yet never been able to. Her inaugural column was about the challenges of engaging in oral sex in public places, but that was not the source of the sensation. The sensational part was a letter her paper published the following week. It was from Mary Ellen's mother, and it was but a single sentence: "Now the entire world knows my daughter is a cocksucker." And, boom, just like that, Mary Ellen had what every columnist needs, which is a personality. Suddenly she was a human being with a mother who was reading her column each week and then sending in letters with words like *cocksucker* in them. It was a brilliant shortcut, really, and it went a long way to make up for the fact that Mary Ellen is not much of a writer. You might think I'm just being catty, but it's the truth. When it comes down to it, she's just one of those girls who likes to write about how good she is in bed.

Which is why Olivia hated her even more than I did. Olivia

thought she had cornered that particular market, at least in Philadelphia. I should probably take a moment here to draw what will undoubtedly seem like an overly fine distinction. Olivia is a writer who answers letters about sex, while Mary Ellen writes columns about her life, and it just so happens that her life includes an awful lot of sex. As I said, this probably seems like a fine point, but without giving away where all this is headed, you should know that it is still rare to see two regularly recurring sex columns in a single alternative newspaper, although God knows the people in power are eager to find a way to do so without appearing to be too tacky, too bottom-feeding, too pandering. I suppose they don't want to appear to be too pandering because it might draw attention to the fact that that's what they're actually doing. It took me a very long time to realize that the ads in the back of the newspaper I wrote for were for prostitutes. I'm not sure what I thought these ladies were selling; I just didn't think prostitutes were allowed to advertise. Well, whether or not they are, the truth is they do. In fact, the real boom time for alternative newspapers in the United States were the years between the deregulation of 976 numbers and the emergence of Internet porn.

One of the problems with writing a humor column on deadline is that occasionally it doesn't quite go off. Now, when it is your job to write a column, and it doesn't go off, and you end up just throwing something down that begins one place and winds up someplace entirely unrelated, it doesn't bother you nearly as much as it should, largely because you are so relieved to open up the newspaper the next day and see actual words there instead of the enormous gaping empty white space that, the night before, you felt certain you'd be reduced to running. You did it. You pulled it out. And the fact that what you pulled out happened to be trivial or self-indulgent or embarrassing or idiotic — well, you figure you're too close to judge. There is something to be said for that sort of creativity, creativity with a gun at your head, in that you end up writing things which under normal circumstances you never would have written, and that can produce the occasional jewel. Most of the time, though, it doesn't. Most of the time it produces something other than a jewel. And I suppose my real problem with Mary Ellen was that reading her column reminded me of that fact, reading her column reminded me that the line between refreshing and shameless is dangerously thin. I would read Mary Ellen's column, and I would think: there is a silly girl writing silly things.

And yet. And yet, she is not a good person either. That is the other part of it. She is neither good nor nice. I realize I probably care too much about being good and nice. I also realize that there are many other qualities that a person ought to develop, that goodness and niceness should probably be beaten out of people like me, and perhaps I would be better off if I were a little more bad and mean, but still. Like my issue with any woman who doesn't give a rat's ass about being good or nice, my real problem with Mary Ellen was simply this: she scared me. I did not understand the rules she was playing by, and I secretly believed she was playing with no rules whatsoever.

"What did you judge?" Mary Ellen asked me when she saw me walk in.

"Pie," I said. "Fourteen pies, actually. You?"

"Muffins," she said. "They gave us the girl food."

"Matt ate twelve cheesesteaks," I said.

Mary Ellen twirled a long strand of her blond hair around a forefinger. "I'm sorry about you and Tom," she said.

I nodded my head.

"Kate feels horrible about everything," she said.

It took me a moment to take this in.

"You know her?"

"She's a friend."

"Of course," I said. "Of course. She would be."

"She really doesn't believe in this sort of thing," said Mary Ellen. "I told her months ago that it was really not cool. You know, not cool."

My head was starting to spin.

"She says Tom only says really nice things about you," said Mary Ellen.

"Yeah, well. Excuse me," I said. "I have someplace to be."

I headed for the ladies room in a daze. It took me a minute to put all the pieces together, even though there were only about three pieces and they fit together quite plainly. Mary Ellen had known that Tom was sleeping with Kate Pearce before I did. And — in some ways this was even worse — she wanted me to *know* that she'd known. It wasn't enough that I'd been humiliated without my knowledge. She felt the need to bring my humiliation to my attention. I could just picture her, reading my column each week, columns in which I smugly documented the process of moving in with Tom, and buying a couch with Tom, my all-around happiness with Tom, and the whole time she knew that Tom was fucking Kate Pearce behind my back. I felt sick. I honestly wanted to die. A part of me could handle the fact that Kate knew — I mean, I had plenty of reasons to be angry with Kate, and the fact that she knew about her affair with Tom before I did fell reasonably low on the list — but Mary Ellen! My arch enemy! A woman who wished me nothing but ill! I was mortified. And I honestly couldn't believe that Tom had put me in this situation. I realize this sounds crazy, but a part of me could understand how Tom could end up sleeping with Kate Pearce, and even how he could keep seeing her for several months behind my back, but that he could do it knowing that Mary Ellen would find out, knowing that his doing so would humiliate me like this — that seemed almost impossible. How was it possible?

He must have really hated me. I sat there, on the toilet seat, tears rolling down my face, as I lit on that thought. *Tom must have really hated me.* That was the only explanation I could come up with that made any sense. That was the only way things could possibly add up. Just thinking those words in my head, just thinking that *sentence* made me so sad I could hardly breathe. What had I done to make him hate me so much? I wondered. And how come I didn't see it? I mean, a part of me could understand how Tom could hide an infidelity, I could sort of appreciate how all the lies stacked on top of each other like bricks — but how on earth did he hide the hate?

The door to the bathroom swung open, and I could hear voices. Two women I didn't know came in, talking about a sous chef at Treetops who had apparently tried to influence the judging. I did my best to calm down. This was not the time or the place. I would have to do this later, someplace other than a refurbished train station brimming with Philadelphia's culinary and media elite.

The women left. I unlocked the stall and went over to one of the sinks. I splashed cold water on my face and carefully blotted it with a paper towel. Why am I always having my big emotional moments in bathrooms? I asked myself. A good shrink could make something of this sort of pattern, although I'm not sure I want to know what they'd come up with. I wondered if it would still be considered repression. I suppose feeling things in bathroom stalls is less repressed than not feeling them at all. I looked at my face in the mirror over the sink and tried to think about Henry, to keep myself from thinking any more about Tom. Henry, who had proven himself to be a worthy distraction, Henry, who for about sixty seconds I thought I was in love with even though I really wasn't, but who nonetheless I was interested in going to bed with again, later that night if at all possible, only now I saw that there were two problems with that plan. The first was the scene earlier that day in his office. The second was that now I looked like a raccoon. I opened up my purse and calmly set about fixing my face.

By the time I finished in the bathroom, the party was in full swing. The lights were low enough that I thought I could pass for normal.

"Jesus, Alison," Matt said when he saw me. "What happened to you?"

"Is it that bad?"

"It's hardly noticeable," said Matt. He grabbed two glasses of wine from a roaming waitress and handed me one. "Here. Drink."

"Thank you."

"You're not still upset about Tom, are you?"

I nodded my head yes.

"Talk to me."

We leaned up against a thick pillar in the middle of the room. We watched the rest of the partygoers milling by while we talked.

"It's like I was two people in the relationship," I said. "Part of me was down there, in the middle of it, and another part of me was evaluating everything from a distance."

"Like Napoleon watching the battlefield from the top of a hill," said Matt.

"Exactly," I said. "And there was going to be a winner, and there was going to be a loser."

"How do you mean?"

"If we got married, that meant I won," I said, "and if we didn't, then Tom won."

"What did he win?"

"He got the best years of my life, and then he got to go start over with somebody else," I said.

"For a person with high self-esteem, you have awfully low self-esteem."

I shrugged my shoulders. "Then I realized a man can *always* go start over with somebody else. He can do it when he's eighty. So, really, the only way I can win is if he's dead. If he's with me for a long time and then he dies. Then I win."

"Marry me," said Matt.

"I realize I'm insane," I said. "That's something, right?"

"I mean it," he said. "Marry me. Although I might want to still be allowed to date girls like her."

"Girls like who?" I said.

Matt motioned to a woman wearing a fringy halter top. She looked Matt up and down and then coolly turned her back to him. It was one of those flawless, bony-yet-fleshy backs, but still.

"She's like one of those statues that guards a Japanese temple," Matt said to me. "Her right hand is up here, going stop. But her left hand is down below, coyly beckoning me in."

"Is that what that was?"

"Yes. But I don't have time for that tonight," said Matt. "Tonight I'm going to pick the low-hanging fruit."

Olivia walked over to us, carrying a tiny plastic plate heaped with wontons. I cocked an eyebrow at Matt.

"Not that low-hanging," said Matt.

"What?" Olivia said.

"Nothing," I said.

"I don't want to alarm you," Olivia said to me. She motioned to one of the risers that had been set up in the back. Sid Hirsch and Mary Ellen were huddled together at a cocktail table, deep in conversation.

"Which one of us should be worried?" I said to Olivia.

"That I don't know."

It wasn't until much later that I finally saw Henry. He was standing at a makeshift bar that had been set up alongside the fish market, and he was talking to a woman who threw her head back whenever she laughed. She had an unbelievably long neck. I couldn't stop staring at it. That's what I was doing, in fact, when Henry caught my eye: I was staring at this woman's neck. I watched as he touched her arm, and then walked over to where I was standing.

"Hello," I said.

"Hi there," said Henry.

"Your date has a disturbingly long neck," I said.

"Her?" Henry said. He looked over his shoulder at the woman. "She's not my date."

"Well, if you like her, you should try not to look at it," I said, "because once you look at it you won't be able to stop. It's hypnotizing."

Henry looked at her, and, as if on cue, she did the neck thing.

"Mesmerizing," he said.

"That's the word," I said.

"Alison," said Henry.

"Yes?"

He smiled with only half of his mouth and didn't say anything.

"What is it?" I said.

He took a breath. "I can't handle you."

I just stood there.

"I've thought about it, and I've decided that I can't," said Henry.

"Oh," I said.

"I'd like it if there wasn't any weirdness," he said.

He'd like it if there wasn't any weirdness.

"Not a problem," I said. I smiled, in an attempt to indicate my ability to not be weird.

"Good."

He put his hand on my right shoulder. He squeezed it. And then he went back to the bar and his drink and the girl with the neck.

I went home that night and wrote a column about Romantic Market Value. I'd been meaning to write that particular column for years, but I'd been holding off, for two reasons. First of all, it wasn't my idea. I'd stolen it from someplace and added it to my repertoire, and in the process I'd changed it around a bit, and the whole thing had happened so long ago that I couldn't remember exactly where I'd stolen it from or just how much I'd changed it, which is the sort of thing that's okay to do in life but makes me nervous to do in print. Second of all, it's sort of offensive. After I turned in the column the next morning, Olivia barreled over to my desk and said, "What are you saying? Men would like me more if I were *thinner* and *prettier*?" It's more complicated than that, of course — but yes. That's what I was saying. Romantic Market Value is just that: a person's value in the romantic marketplace. It's that thing that makes you think two people go together, that they fit, that one isn't going to run off and find someone better, because they're both more or less the same, that is, they have roughly the same RMV. And the girl with the neck had, objectively speaking, a higher RMV than me, because she was beautiful. I've come to terms with the fact that I am, beautywise, not everybody's cup of tea, and for the most part I'm fine with it (it's enough that I am some people's cup of tea), but it does lower my Romantic Market Value, and there are times when it really pisses me off.

It was an easy column to write. I simply crafted into paragraphs various things I'd infuriated my friends with over the years. The infuriating part, in case you haven't figured it out yet, is that men and women's Romantic Market Value is based on different things; women are valued for youth and beauty, men for wealth and power. This is insulting to members of both sexes, but — as women are quick to point out — it is not *equally* insulting to members of both sexes. And one is not exactly overwhelmed by the roar of complaints coming from young, goodlooking men.

Anyhow, like I said, this was one of my pet theories, and it felt good to finally get it down on paper, but later, as I read it over one last time while I was lying in bed, I was struck by something really quite odd. I suddenly saw, with a sort of otherworldly clarity, that this was stuff I actually believed. I believed it way down in the place where I was supposed to believe in love. And I'd like to be one of those people who live in the moment, who don't plot and plan and scheme and control, but I don't know if my brain could take it. What on earth would I think about all day long? My brain plays with relationships. That's what it does. I see a happy couple and I immediately want all the facts. How did they meet? How does it work? Who loves who more? Who has the power?

Because that, in the end, is what I was talking about — power. *Who has the power?* And I suppose the thing I'd always liked most about the concept of Romantic Market Value was that it was an attempt to quantify the thing I found most fascinating. I liked the almost mathematical logic of it all, the simple fact that after a while in certain relationships, the power imbalance becomes so extreme that there needs to be a rebalancing of the scales. But the truth is, power is much more elusive than that. I'll tell you who has the power. The person who loves less has the power. The person who is most willing to leave has the power. I'll tell you something else. Infidelity is power. No matter what has gone on in a relationship, the person who fucks around takes all the power back.

All along I'd been thinking that my problem was that Tom had left me, but I see now that it's possible my problem was much more fundamental. Maybe love shouldn't be about power. Maybe confusing the two was getting me into trouble.

Thirteen

"THE OLDER I GET, THE FURTHER AWAY FROM THE URINAL I start unzipping my pants," Sid Hirsch said to me as he walked into his office.

It was late on Friday afternoon, and I was already inside Sid's office, waiting for him. I'd been summoned. Sid summoned one to his office and then tended to disappear, because he liked to make an entrance. He walked over to his desk and sat down on top of it with his legs folded Indian-style. "Yoga," he explained. He took a long, cleansing breath and then looked me in the eye and said, "We have a problem."

Oh shit, I thought. Sid knows about me and Henry. How could he know about me and Henry? I considered the possibility that Sid subscribed to Olivia's theory that if you think two people are sleeping together, they are (with the corollary that if you think a person is gay, he is).

"What is it?" I said.

"I heard about what happened with you and your boyfriend," said Sid.

"Oh."

"And I'm really sorry about it."

"It's okay," I said. "I'm going to be fine."

"Of course you'll be fine," he said.

"What's the problem?" I said.

Sid pressed his hands into a power teepee and rested his chin on his fingertips. "Your column was about a nice girl trying to trick some poor schlub into marrying her. There was an arc there. We were all waiting for the ring. Now the guy turns out to be a complete shit. Fine. Write that last column. That's the end of the story."

I just looked at him.

"You're giving Mary Ellen my column," I said.

"Number one, it isn't your column. My paper, my column," Sid said. "Number two, yes I am."

Now, I had given some thought to what I would do when I was through working at the paper. I had devoted a great deal of time to fantasizing about it, in fact. There were several versions of this fantasy, the gist of all of which involved me getting paid a great deal of money for something I'd written on the side. Sometimes it was a book. Sometimes it was a screenplay. Sometimes it was a book that sold to the movies and I was begged to write the screenplay. The fact that I wasn't actually doing any writing on the side did surprisingly little to interfere with this particular fantasy.

Someday I would, and when I did, the fantasy would be there, waiting for me. But this particular scenario was one I had never considered. It had never entered my mind that I would be fired.

"I can't believe this," I said.

"Don't take this personally," he said.

"I'm being fired, Sid. It feels personal."

"It's not about you," he said. "It's the trend."

"What trend is this exactly?"

Sid slid off of his desk and began to pace around behind it. "You know," he said. "Hot girls in bars talking about dildos. Unashamed of their sexuality. They are woman, hear them roar."

"I'm a woman," I said.

"Your column is about a nice girl. People love you, but they don't want to fuck you. I'm speaking metaphorically of course. I'm sure there are plenty of people who'd like to fuck you," Sid said. "I'd fuck you."

"Fuck you, Sid," I said.

He held up his right hand like he was willingly taking the blow.

"This girl is twenty-seven," said Sid. "She's bi-curious. I'm pretty sure her parents are dead."

"Mary Ellen's parents aren't dead," I said. "Her mother sends in those letters."

"Well, she writes like her parents are dead," said Sid. "If she were my daughter, I'd kill myself."

"What about when I start dating new people?" I said. I considered telling Sid about what had happened with Henry — not that it was Henry, simply that I'd already had sex with some-body four times on two separate occasions and I'd be willing to write about it. "I could be more explicit."

"I've thought about that," he said. "It won't work. You can't turn Mary Tyler Moore into a whore and expect people to feel good about it."

I didn't say anything.

"Never mind that it's pathetic," he said. "There's nothing to root for."

"There is something to root for," I said. "Me. People can root for me."

"I'm sorry, Alison. But you've got your whole future in front of you."

"Everyone has their future in front of them, Sid. That's why they call it the future."

I got up to leave.

"I'm going to give you a piece of advice," Sid said.

"What."

Sid picked at a tuft of chest hair that was peeking out of his V-neck. "Move to Pittsburgh."

"Pittsburgh?"

"They have a nice weekly. Smallish. You might have to wait-ress a little on the side. I'll put in a call to the publisher for you. His name is Ed," Sid said. He got a quizzical look on his face. "Ted? I'll look it up."

"Fuck you, Sid," I said. And I left.

* * *

I walked down the hallway in a state of escalating panic. Writing a column for an alternative newspaper is not much to cling to, but it was all I had. And now I didn't have it anymore. I felt completely humiliated. When I got to Henry's office, I found myself looking at the door, which was closed. The irony, of course, of having embarked upon a clandestine affair with one boss and then being fired by the other one because nobody wants to fuck you was not lost on me. (Is that irony? I always get messed up with irony. Even if it is irony, I suppose it becomes considerably less ironic when you toss in the fact that apparently Henry didn't want to fuck me anymore, either. That's no longer irony, really — that's just sad.)

And there was the problem of money. I don't like to get into this particular area, because it reflects so poorly on me, but the truth is that my plan to be paid a great deal of money for something I'd written on the side had had an unfortunate repercussion, which is that I had managed to accumulate a small mountain of credit card debt which I had no conceivable, non-pie-in-the-sky means to pay off. I'd had no possible means to pay it off when I was gainfully employed — now that I'd lost my job, I couldn't see how I'd be able to handle the minimums. Why do they give credit cards to people like me? Why, why, why? My logic at the time of amassing this debt — and perhaps the word *logic* is ill chosen — was that I was like one of those renegade filmmakers who make entire movies using nothing but their credit cards as financing. Only I had skipped over the whole "making a movie" part. I'd gone to Morocco. I'd bought shoes.

When I reached the editorial office, I opened the door. Matt was sitting behind my desk, reading over my column.

"Camilla Parker Bowles," Matt said, without looking up.

"What?" I said.

"If your Romantic Market Value theory is correct, how do you explain Prince Charles and Camilla Parker Bowles?"

"I don't really know, Matt."

Matt stood up and walked towards me. He fixed me with a serious look.

"What happened to you?"

"Sid just fired me," I said.

"Impossible."

I nodded my head.

"Not possible."

"I'm afraid it is."

"Oh my God. This is madness," Matt said. "If you can get fired, I could be, I don't know, summarily executed in the hallway. Did he say why?"

I thought back to my conversation with Sid. "Apparently I don't write about dildos often enough."

"Which is true. Completely true," Matt said. "Although I didn't realize that was a fireable offense."

"Neither did I."

"You could sue him," said Matt.

"Nobody would believe it," I said. "I hardly believe it, and I was in the room at the time."

"Let's get out of here."

We walked downstairs and stood outside on the sidewalk.

After a minor consultation, we headed towards his place. I went over everything that happened in Sid's office, while Matt made the appropriate interjections. I started out really upset, and then I got incredibly angry, but by the time we reached Matt's place I felt almost normal again. Matt has this effect on me, and I have never been able to figure out why.

"I'm going to cook for you," Matt said when we got inside.

"I didn't know you cooked."

"I cook. Of course I cook. I only know how to make one thing, but I do it better than anybody else."

"What's the one thing?"

"Eggs Florentine."

"I've never had eggs Florentine."

"Do you know what's in eggs Florentine?"

"No idea."

"Good."

Matt cleared off a space at the kitchen counter for me, and I sat down on one of his bar stools and started picking at a bowl of pistachio nuts. He opened up a bottle of red wine and poured two big glasses. He handed one to me and then raised his glass to make a toast.

"Can I tell you my new theory?" I said.

"Of course."

"I think that toasting is the new prayer," I said. "It's the socially acceptable way of indulging the impulse for communal prayer. That's why nobody just says 'cheers' anymore."

"In that case," Matt said. "Holy-Jesus-Mary-and-Joseph-help-us-dear-God-help-us."

We clinked and drank.

Matt started chopping a big bunch of basil. "You know," he said, "this is going to be the best thing that ever happened to you."

"Don't say that," I said.

"Why not?"

"Because it's the kind of thing people say when something really bad happens to you, and it has no basis in reality whatsoever," I said. "Plenty of bad things happen that are just plain bad, and people never recover from them, and their life never gets back to where it was, and it's impossible to tell at this point whether or not this is that kind of thing or the other kind of thing."

"The other kind of thing?"

"The bad thing that becomes the good thing."

"I think you'll recover from this," said Matt.

"Thank you."

"And I think you'll recover from the Tom thing," he said.

"I might recover from that, or I might not," I said. I took a big swallow of wine. "You can't really understand it, because you don't have to worry about getting too old to have babies."

Matt looked up from his chopping. "Well, I'd like to have kids before I'm too old to molest them."

I laughed at this. I couldn't help myself.

"See, that's a good sign. Your life is falling apart, and yet you're capable of laughing at molestation jokes. All is not lost."

"A lot is lost."

"But not all."

I went upstairs to use the bathroom. Matt lives in one of those row houses that was built in the middle of the nineteenth century, when people in Philadelphia were apparently very small. The kitchen is in the basement, the bedroom is on top, and in between there is a living room. It reminds me of a dollhouse in an extreme state of disrepair.

When I came back down, we sat down at the table to eat. Matt's eggs Florentine turned out to be indistinguishable from a tomato and basil omelet.

"Do you mind if I get drunk tonight?" I said.

"Why would I mind?"

"I just like to warn whoever I'm with when I'm planning to get drunk that I'm planning to get drunk. I don't want them to think it's an accident."

"You are consciously surrendering consciousness."

"Yes," I said. "Which I think might be classified as alcoholic behavior, but I'm not sure."

"I went out with this woman who was in AA, and according to her, everything I did was alcoholic behavior."

"What kinds of things?"

"Oh, I don't know," said Matt. "Getting drunk all the time."

I smiled.

"Not trusting life. You have to trust life, she kept saying to me. Trust your life. And, I mean, if my life proves one thing, it's that life should not be trusted."

"What's wrong with your life?"

Matt leaned back in his chair and closed his eyes for a moment. "Okay," he said. "Last weekend, I had to go to my aunt Mitzie's funeral."

"I'm sorry," I said.

"No, it's fine," said Matt. "Not for her of course, she's dead. But I'm fine."

"Good."

"Anyhow, my uncle, who's seventy-six and not in the greatest health himself, is all alone now. My aunt had been taking care of him, but then one day — pffft — she just goes in her sleep. So, we're at the synagogue. And my uncle is sitting in the front in his wheelchair, and during the entire ceremony you can hear him moaning, 'I just want to die. Please, somebody help me die. I don't want to live anymore, I just want to die.' It was unbelievably depressing. I mean, the man has no kids, he's really sick, and his wife of fifty years just dropped dead in the middle of the night. She was in bed when it happened, so I suppose she didn't technically *drop* dead, since she was lying down at the time —"

"Anyway."

"*Anyway.* Then we all drive out to the cemetery. The casket is in front, about to be lowered into the ground, and people are saying the things they say in that situation, only they almost can't because the wind is blowing really hard and there's so much wailing coming from my uncle. 'I just want to die, please, somebody, anybody, help me die. I can't go on anymore. Put me out of my misery.' Then, on a dime really, he turns to the attendant who's been pushing his wheelchair and says, 'I'm cold. I want to go sit in the car.'" Matt took a big gulp of wine. "Which sums up my psychological situation perfectly. I want to die, but I'm also cold, and I want to go sit in the car."

"That's a good story."

"I know. I'm thinking of using it when I'm out on dates," said Matt. "How do I come off?"

"Funny. Perceptive," I said. "Slightly unbalanced."

I got up to get a glass of water. I stood at the sink, filling it up. I looked over my shoulder at Matt, who was sitting at the table. He had a look on his face.

"What?" I said.

"Your ass is looking good these days," said Matt.

"Don't say that," I said.

"Why not? It's a compliment."

"I just don't like the idea that somebody I know is monitoring my ass," I said. "Good or bad. I just don't like it."

"Fine. I'll discontinue my entire Alison's-ass monitoring program," he said.

I sat back down at the table.

"Why don't you monitor Olivia's ass instead."

"Oh, I do."

Later, we went upstairs and sat on the couch. Matt had opened a second bottle of wine, which we were most of the way through. I tucked the edges of an afghan under my legs.

"There's nothing worse than a Jewish funeral," Matt said, "because we have no afterlife."

"You must have something," I said.

"When I was a kid I asked my dad, Dad, when I die, will I go to heaven? No, he says. Jews don't believe in heaven. Well, what do we believe in instead? I asked him. Nothing, the man tells me."

"He really said that? Nothing?"

"Nothing," said Matt. "I was nine years old at the time. Which means that the existential crisis brought on by that 'nothing' has passed the quarter-century mark. And most of the time they manage to gloss over it. But at a funeral, you know, the question's gonna come up."

"So what do they say?"

He swirled the wine around in his glass. "Apparently Aunt Mitzie is going to live on in my memory. Which is unfortunate for her, because I spend very little time thinking about dead people," Matt said. "You're Catholic, right?"

"Protestant, actually."

"Same thing," he said. "At least you get heaven. At least you get angels and tiny harps and 'follow the white light.'"

In point of fact, I don't think we get to follow the white light, but that seemed to be quibbling, so I didn't say anything.

"Even if it's not true," said Matt, "sometimes it would be nice to think it was true."

We were both quiet for a moment. My head was starting to spin from all the wine.

"So," Matt said. He got a very serious look on his face. "Wanna fuck?"

I gave a short, surprised laugh.

"No," I said. "But thanks for asking."

"I'm nothing if not a gentleman," said Matt. "Have some more wine. You might change your mind."

"I think I need to sleep," I said. I remembered something Matt had said about the girl with four cats. "I might get in your bed and sleep with you but not sleep with you."

"I knew you were that girl," said Matt.

We went upstairs. Matt loaned me a T-shirt and a pair of boxers. I went into the bathroom to change, and then I got into bed. Matt has a surprisingly comfortable bed. It's huge, and it takes up so much space that when you want to get in or out you can't come in from the sides, because the walls are so close; you have to climb up from the foot. Matt turned out the light and crawled up into bed beside me. He put his arms around me, and after a few minutes I started to drift off to sleep.

"When you were in grade school," Matt said, "were you one of those girls who, when you loaned somebody a pencil, said, 'make sure I get that back'?"

"*No.*"

"Just checking."

Fourteen

I MET TOM HATHAWAY AT A DINNER PARTY GIVEN BY MY FRIEND Nina Peeble. Nina used to be my very best friend, and then for a while she wasn't my friend at all, but by the time she threw the dinner party where I met Tom, we were friends again. I remember thinking that night when I got home how happy I was that Nina and I were friends again, because if we hadn't made up I wouldn't have been invited to her dinner party, and if I hadn't gone to her dinner party I wouldn't have met the man I was going to marry, and if I hadn't met the man I was going to marry at that particular party I quite possibly never would have met him at all, and the rest of my life would have been wasted, searching for him.

"I don't know," Nina said the next day, when I called her up and asked about Tom.

"What's wrong with him?" I said.

"Nothing," said Nina.

"What is it," I said.

"That thing with his nose doesn't bug you?" she said.

"What's wrong with his nose?" I said.

"If you didn't notice it, then that's great," said Nina.

"Notice what?" I said.

"Nothing," Nina said. "I'll see what I can do."

Two weeks later, Tom Hathaway called me and asked me out to dinner. Nina had arranged the whole thing. It's impossible to convey, really, just how good Nina Peeble is at that sort of thing. She managed to fix up her brother Jack with an OB/GYN he saw on the *Today* show doing a segment on perimenopause; six months later they were engaged. Anyway, it was very kind of her, and it was certainly more than I had a right to expect, given our complex history.

It is my belief that all successful female friendships fall into the same basic paradigm: one person gets to be the girl and the other one has to be the boy. I was just about to claim that this has nothing whatsoever to do with lesbianism, but now that I think about it, I don't think that's true; what I'm talking about, in fact, is a nonsexual version of the same agreement you see in lesbian couples, where the girl is the girl and the boy is the boy and both parties are more or less fine with it. Now, the interesting thing about me is that in some friendships I'm the girl and in others I'm the boy. With Bonnie, for example, I'm the girl — mainly because she's married and has three kids and isn't really interested in being the girl anymore; and with my friend Angie, I'm the girl — because Angie is much too sensible to want to be the girl; but with Nina Peeble, I'm the boy. I always have been. It was clear to me that if Nina and I were going to be friends I'd have to be the boy before I even met her, because I happened to see the inside of her underwear drawer. She was assigned to be my roommate my freshman year in college, and by the time I showed up on move-in day she was already settled in and off to the campus bookstore, and while I was looking for a place to put my stuff I pulled open what turned out to be her underwear drawer. There were rows and rows and rows of perfectly folded pastel underpants, lovingly arranged with little dividers and satin sachets and tiny boxes holding God knows what, and I knew immediately that this was a woman with whom I could not compete.

The problem with this arrangement, of course, is that the person who is forced to be the boy eventually starts to resent it. My resentment towards Nina took eight years to flower, and when it did, it took the following form: I slept over at her old boyfriend's apartment and almost had sex with him and then I called her up and told her about it. Of course, I wasn't conscious that that was my motivation at the time; I thought I really liked him. His name was Andy Bass, and he was four hundred and fifty pages deep into a novel he was writing about a twelfth-century pilgrim who was journeying to Santiago de Compostela with a scallop shell tied around his neck, and his apartment was piled with books on monastic orders and medieval architecture and the Black Death, and the night I slept over I had to wear his ski gloves to bed because his heat had been turned off by the utility company. We stayed up most of the night, making out and talking about Rilke and Foucault, and then at six o'clock the next morning he jumped out of bed and ran outside and moved his car to the opposite curb to avoid getting a parking ticket from the street sweepers. For some reason I found him appealing. Anyhow, it was a stupid thing to do, getting involved with him in the first place, and when I told Nina she was understandably upset (although, to be fair, Nina and Andy hadn't seen each other in four years and were by all accounts *completely* over — by that point in her life, Nina Peeble was more or less exclusively dating investment bankers and future congressmen), and, as a result, she refused to speak to me for two years. But then, just as suddenly as it began, it ended. Nina called me on my birthday and told me she missed me and she forgave me and she wanted to be friends again, and she was throwing one of her dinner parties, and would I like to come along. I said I would; and I went; and there was Tom.

I managed to create a rather elaborate hypothetical personality for Tom based on the two anecdotes he shared with the table at the party. The first one was about some legal work he was doing for three orphans who'd been abused by their foster mother and fed nothing but Wonder Bread and ketchup soup. The second had to do with six weeks he'd spent in Alaska, alone, kayaking through the interior. Well. Here was a man who cared about orphans. Here was a man who wasn't afraid of bears. Here was a man who knew how to catch a salmon by tying a fishing line to the back of his kayak. I don't ever expect to find myself in a situation in which I need a man who can catch a salmon by tying a fishing line to the back of his kayak, but still. You never know.

By the time Nina Peeble persuaded Tom to take me out to dinner, I was out of my mind, really, with fantasies of the two of us kayaking through untamed wilderness with our two biological children and the adorable, freckle-faced orphans we'd adopted, and I was convinced that it would show. My only hope, it seemed to me, was to pretend that I wasn't interested in him at all — I figured the two poles would cancel each other out and I'd end up seeming relatively normal. So, when Tom showed up at my front door for our date, I searched hard for flaws. He was as tall as I remembered, and his shoulders were just as broad, but Nina had been right about his nose — it veered off a little to the left. Nina would never consider dating a man with a nose that veered, but Nina could afford to be picky. I'd given up on picky. It could be argued that I'd skipped over picky altogether — how else could you explain my nineteen months with Gil-the-homosexual? — but the truth is that Gil had been the classic Good On Paper boyfriend, and in my mid-twenties pickiness I'd selected him over all sorts of more obviously flawed yet heterosexual options. Anyhow, Tom's nose is what keeps him from being conventionally good-looking, and I've always been grateful for that. It's just noticeable enough to make you think he might have encountered some sort of trauma in the birth canal. (Years later, I happened to mention a theory to my therapist Janis Finkle — that maybe the reason Tom was feeling suffocated in our relationship was because he had gotten stuck in the birth canal — and Janis said to me, "Maybe he feels suffocated in your relationship because you're suffocating him.")

"What the hell happened last night?" Nina said when she called me the next morning.

"What do you mean?" I said.

"Tom thinks you can't stand him," said Nina.

"I was trying to seem disinterested," I said.

"Well, you succeeded."

"Shit."

"He said you kept staring at his nose."

"Oh, God."

"I told you it was bad," Nina said. "You didn't believe me."

"I really don't mind it," I said.

"A nose belongs in the center of the face," Nina said.

"I think I'm in love with him."

"Oh, dear," Nina said. "Let me see what I can do."

So Nina went to work again, and Tom called me again, and we went out to dinner again, and afterwards, in a particularly valiant effort to not appear disinterested, I invited him back to my apartment and went to bed with him. This was not exactly my style, but look at what my style had gotten me: I'd had a single gay lover who was walking around with the last name of a Chinese woman who'd dumped him for an Argentinean salsa instructor. Perhaps it was time for a new approach. So when Tom walked me home, I invited him up, and just as I was unlocking the door to my apartment building he put his hands firmly on my shoulders and turned me around. And then he kissed me.

"You know, rats won't mate with each other if they don't like the way the other one tastes," said Tom.

"How come?" I said.

"That's how they tell if they're a good genetic match," he said. "If they like the way the other one tastes, then they're a good match."

He kissed me again.

"I like the way you taste," said Tom.

"I like the way you taste, too," I said.

I realize that that doesn't sound at all romantic, but you're going to have to trust me on this one. You have to trust me here because it's hard, really hard, to try to explain what it is exactly that made you fall in love with a person. The parts that make you fall out of love, that's easy. The treachery and the infidelity and the lies and the minor cruelties — those things are considerably easy to get across. But I couldn't in good conscience leave out the stuff about our first kiss and the rats tasting each other, because it's representative of an entire side of Tom that I quickly came to love, which I think of as his Mr. Wizard side. For the first few months of our relationship, in fact, it seemed like whenever we weren't having sex, Tom was explaining something to me. How they make a seedless watermelon seedless. How those clocks that plug into a potato work. Why our kids would have blue eyes but not necessarily blond hair. One time, when we drove out to Lancaster for the weekend, he walked me out into the middle of an alfalfa field and used the beam of his flashlight to point out the constellations to me, and then we went back to the bed-and-breakfast and had sex in what turned out to be a ninety-year-old wingback chair, which the proprietors proceeded to remove from our room the next morning while we were off having brunch, along with the Oriental rug.

"You know what's weird?" Tom said to me the next morning.

"What?"

"This feels exactly the way it's supposed to feel," Tom said. "In my experience, very few things in life feel exactly the way they're supposed to feel."

"I know what you mean."

"Do you?" he said.

"I do."

"Good," he said. "That means you love me, too."

And I did. I loved him and he loved me, and everything was good for a long, long time. It was a relationship. We were a couple. We did Thanksgiving at his grandparents' house and Christmas at my parents' house and New Year's Eve with our friends Darren and Wendy, and once, early on, we even carved a pumpkin together for Halloween. When people we knew got married, we gave them wedding presents as a unit, and when Sid's wife ended up dead at the bottom of his swimming pool I sent an elegant arrangement of white lilies from the both of us, and my sister's kids called us Auntie Alison and Uncle Tom. I was happy. I was relaxed. But, every so often, something would happen that would remind me that it was all an illusion — no, illusion is the wrong word; it was real, but it was temporary. It was a temporary situation.

Like Tom would decide to buy a new couch.

"What's wrong with your couch?" I said.

"Nothing. I'm just tired of it," said Tom.

"I'm not sure about this one," I said when I saw it in the showroom. (This was the kind of couch you'd see in a showroom.)

"What's the matter with it?" said Tom.

"It doesn't really go with anything," I said.

"It's black," he said. "Black goes with everything."

"Black shoes go with everything," I said. "A black leather couch only goes with, I don't know, Buck Rogers furniture."

"Well, I like it," Tom said.

Tom bought the couch. Next, he brought home a jagged-edged glass-topped coffee table. Then it was a truly horrible entertainment console. Through it all, I kept my mouth shut. I tried not to push. I tried desperately to be the kind of woman who has her shit so completely together that she doesn't even notice that her boyfriend of three years is making a series of high-end home purchasing decisions without so much as considering whether or not said purchases could ever blend in with the tasteful, non-Buck-Rogers furniture she has been slowly accumulating all of her adult life. Any man who doesn't have trouble with commitment is already committed to somebody else, I'd remind myself. Go slow. Give the man his space. The couch can always go in his study.

Still, every so often, something inside me would snap.

"You think you don't have issues, but you do," I said to Tom one day after I got home from therapy.

"What are my issues?" said Tom.

"I'm not going to tell you," I said.

"Give me one issue," said Tom.

"Okay," I said. "Your mother."

"What about my mother?"

I took a deep breath. "You have unresolved feelings of anger towards your mother."

"No, I don't," he said.

"Yes, you do," I said.

"I love my mother," he said.

"You just think you do," I said.

"What is that supposed to mean?" said Tom.

"It means that everybody thinks that they love their mother, and that their mother loves them, until one day they stop to really think about it," I said. "Maybe they do, or maybe they don't, but either way, that's when all their issues start to come up."

"Maybe I don't want my issues to come up."

"That's what's keeping our relationship from going to the next level."

"I like this level," Tom said. "I'm comfortable at this level."

"Because you're angry with your mother."

(Okay, ladies: beware of men who hate their mothers. Because a man who hates his mother will end up hating you. Unfortunately, it is very difficult to get a man to admit that he hates his mother. If you try to draw one out on the subject, he will simply become convinced that *you* hate his mother, which he will then use as an excuse to start hating you when really, the person he hates is, in fact, his mother. But there is an easy way to determine if a man hates his mother. At some point, he will make an offhand comment about her in a tone of voice that is completely unremarkable and yet makes you think, "I wonder if he hates his mother?" and then, trust me, he does.)

In the end, I suppose, what does it matter. Either the man hates his mother, or he loves his mother a little too much. Either he's shut down, so you don't really know what you're dealing with, or he's one of those highly verbal guys who tells you exactly what you're dealing with, and what you're dealing with scares the shit out of you. In the end, what you have is a mess, and your relationship consists of picking around in it. I don't mean to sound so cynical about all this, but I can't help myself. You fall in love with a person because your subconscious likes something about their subconscious, and it isn't until much later that you discover that the thing your subconscious liked was the fact that this person was built to hurt you in precisely the way you most fear.

And the worst part — yes, there is a worst part — is that even when you think you've figured all this out, you haven't. Even when you think you've got it all down, you don't. Even when you think you've gone and made it all conscious, it isn't. You just think it is. Even now, you're probably convinced you've figured this stuff out. You're probably thinking, yes, I used to be just like you, but then I did the work, I ironed out the kinks in my psyche, I found the right person, we do mirroring exercises with each other, we've pulled back our projections, and now I'm happy. And I'm not saying you're not happy. I'm just saying this: beware of happiness. Because happiness tends to be temporary.

I'm telling you all of this for a reason, of course. Nina Peeble predicted the night of the dinner party that Tom would come back, but I didn't believe her, not really, even though I desperately wanted to. I'd lived long enough to know that they always come back to Nina, but they don't always come back to me.

But Tom — surprise surprise — did.

Fifteen

AFTERWARDS, OF COURSE, I TOLD NINA PEEBLE ABOUT TOM showing up on my doorstep, and when I got to the part about him holding the jar of mustard, Nina said, "What an asshole." That threw me a little, to tell you the truth. I mean, I knew Nina would have a problem with Tom cheating on me and leaving me for Kate Pearce and then wanting me to take him back, but that the mustard would bother her so much — that I wasn't prepared for. In fact, it wasn't until Nina made such a big deal about it that it entered my mind that there was more than one way to look at it. At the time, I considered it not exactly charming and not exactly witty, but close enough to both charm and wit to be at least an interesting detail, worthy of sharing. And I didn't even notice the mustard until I had registered the look on Tom's face. You should have seen the man's face. I tried to describe the look on Tom's face to Nina, to mitigate the effect the mustard was having on her, but she wouldn't hear it. "Do you know how easy it is to look sad and guilty when you've done something horrible to a person you love?" Nina said. "It's pretty goddamn easy."

Of course, Nina and I often look at these things differently. One of the reasons it's been so hard to be friends with her over the years is that she says the same thing about every man I ever date. "You can do better" is what she says. Again and again, I can do better. The other thing Nina says that really infuriates me is this: "You don't want to be an old mother." "You can do better" and "You don't want to be an old mother" — what am I doing with a friend who says things like this to me? What do I need to listen to that crap for?

(And since we're on the subject, I would like to go on the record for a moment here and say this: I *do* want to be an old mother. I *very much* want to be an old mother. Women who had their kids early, I do not envy, not in the slightest. And I do not want to hear how my difficulties will be bigger than yours ever were, how I will end up fatter, and saggier, and tireder than you'll ever be. I do not want to hear how young you'll be when your kids go off to college or how old I'll be when mine go. It is the worst kind of crazy female competitiveness, and the truth is I'm sick of it.)

Anyway. Tom on my doorstep. Right. When I woke up that Saturday morning, I was in Matt's bed. It was nice to wake up with another body in the bed, even if it was only Matt. I lay there for a minute or two, staring at the back of his head, and then I got up, got dressed, and quietly let myself out. On my way home, I stopped at the Metropolitan Bakery and picked up an onion bagel and a cup of coffee, and when I rounded the corner onto Delancey, I saw Tom. He was sitting on the top step of the brownstone, and something about the way he was sitting made it immediately clear to me exactly what this was about. Well, well, well, I thought, as I walked across the street and down the sidewalk, towards him. My heart was pounding, and I could feel the blood in my fingertips, but that's all my brain was saying: Well, well, well. What do we have here?

"I miss you, Alison," said Tom.

I didn't say anything.

"I love you," he said.

I just looked at him.

"I can't live without you," he said.

"Apparently you can," I said. I was kind of proud of this, so I said it again. "Apparently," I said, "you can."

This is one of the trickiest parts of this whole story. What makes it tricky is trying to explain to you why I didn't immediately crack one of my landlady's terra-cotta flowerpots over his head. I mean, the man had walked out on me in the middle of a dinner party and told me *over the phone* that he was in love with somebody else — and suddenly he was back, sitting on my stoop, holding a jar of mustard. It was as if the past two weeks had existed in a sort of time warp, like he had gotten tripped up in the time-space continuum, only now here he was, home again, heidi ho, and he had mustard! Come on, little Miss Alison, I can hear you saying. Do not listen to what this man has to say. Do not give him the time of day.

Still, you must understand that I'd been waiting for this moment, and I wanted to see just how it would play out.

"I'm so sorry, Alison."

"I warned you about her," I said.

"I know you did."

"You wouldn't listen to me."

"It was a mistake. A huge, huge mistake."

"Do you still love her?"

"Alison."

"Do you?"

"I love you," said Tom. "I need you. I'm so sorry."

I folded my arms in front of my chest.

"No," said Tom. "No, I don't love her. I didn't ever really love her."

I sat down a few steps below Tom. I took my bagel out of the paper bag and unwrapped it and began quite methodically to scrape off the cream cheese with a plastic knife, until there was only the thinnest possible layer of it left. Even at the time, I remember thinking that this was kind of a cool thing to do, to start in on my bagel like nothing particularly monumental was going on. I think now that something in me felt like Tom had denied me the courtesy of a real breakup by breaking up with me over the phone, and I was going to deny him whatever drama he wanted to get going here. Still, I must admit that I felt a certain satisfaction. I had, at that moment, no earthly idea what I was going to do about all of this, but I'd be lying if I said I wasn't just a little bit pleased.

"I had sex with somebody, too," I finally said. "While you were gone, I mean."

I took a big bite out of my bagel.

"I'm up to three," I said.

I looked up at Tom. "I'm not sure I'm stopping at three."

Tom nodded his head thoughtfully.

"Alison?"

"Um-hm?"

"I'd like to move back in."

I swallowed. "I seriously doubt that's going to happen."

"Please, Alison," said Tom. "Please."

For a significant portion of our relationship, I did not want to move in with Tom and Tom did not want to move in with me, and everything was fine. I didn't want to move in with Tom because I wanted him to propose to me first, and Tom didn't want to move in with me because he didn't want to move in with me. Three and a half years passed in this fashion. Then I decided to lower my sights. "Once he's lived with me he won't be able to live without me" was my thinking. I can't claim to know what Tom was thinking, although Bonnie and Cordelia and I have enjoyed hours and hours of empty speculation about it, which I will kindly spare you. At best, he viewed it as a major concession. He said it was like the Jews offering to give the Palestinians the entire state of Israel. It was, now that I think about it, the very strength of his resistance to the idea that made it feel like such a victory when he finally agreed.

In the end, the reason Tom moved in with me was not because he wanted to, or in order to save money on rent, or even to make me happy. It was because his best friend Darren decided to have a baby. Darren and Tom had gone to Dartmouth together, and they both ended up in Philadelphia after law school, and they were really quite close. They were like girlfriends, really, always having long lunches together and talking on the phone, although it strikes me just now that some of those lunches with Darren might have in fact been lunches with Kate — even now I hate this, the not knowing, the piecing together — but even so, Darren and Tom were close. Darren met his wife Wendy two weeks after Tom met me. Six months later, Darren and Wendy moved in together and Tom and I kept dating. Then they got married, and Tom and I kept dating. Then Darren and Wendy decided to have a baby. They started having sex on day ten, day twelve, day fourteen, and day sixteen. If the four of us happened to have a dinner scheduled for one of their sex days we had to eat late, because Wendy didn't like to have sex on a full stomach. I suppose if I had been looking for signs of trouble that would have been a pretty good place to start, but I wasn't looking for signs of trouble. In fact, I remember thinking that all this was good for Tom, that watching Darren step so easily from life stage to life stage might make him realize that he could just relax and trust the river of life. It seemed to be working, too, because a few months into Darren and Wendy's baby-making effort, Tom told me he wanted to try living together — that's the way he put it, I remember quite clearly, that "try" dangling out there like a threat — and I said yes.

Tom and I found a cute little apartment on the part of Delancey Street you can find apartments on and we moved in. Darren and Wendy brought over red wine and Chinese food our first night, and the four of us ate out of cartons on the living room floor and argued about where to put the couch. The river of life was flowing. Three months later, Darren came home early from work and walked into the bathroom and found Wendy sitting on the toilet seat holding a pregnancy test stick in her hand. It was blue. When Wendy saw Darren, she burst into tears. Then Darren burst into tears. He was under the impression they were having a beautiful moment, but they weren't.

Darren rang our doorbell later that night and told us the news. Wendy was finally pregnant, but she wanted to have an abortion. Tom and I were shocked. We were stunned. They'd been trying to get pregnant for eight months! Eight months of perfunctory, pre-dinner, baby-making sex, and suddenly Wendy decides she wants an abortion. Darren came inside and sat down at our kitchen table and the three of us started drinking. He kept going on about how Wendy wanted to kill his baby. On and on, how it was his baby too, and what right did she have, and I sat there, nodding, fetching bottles of Rolling Rock from the refrigerator, and I didn't say the one thing that was slowly becoming so completely clear to me that it was impossible for me to say anything else.

"Well, obviously it's not Darren's baby," I said to Tom later on, while we were getting ready for bed.

"What are you talking about?" said Tom.

"Wendy went to Acapulco on that business trip," I said.

"So?" said Tom.

"Six weeks ago," I said. "I remember because it was the weekend of your birthday."

"So?"

"She missed her flight and had to stay longer." I looked at Tom to see if he was getting it; he wasn't. "Remember how much longer?" Tom shook his head no. "Two extra days," I said, and I made a gesture, the sort of open-palmed, two-handed gesture one would use to indicate the obviousness of a particular conclusion.

"Wendy missed an airplane six weeks ago and that means this," Tom said. He did the gesture.

"That baby was going to come out habla-ing Español," I said.

"You're crazy," he said.

"It's not even a baby," I said, "it's a bambino." I stood there, desperately trying to remember more of my high school Spanish, but before I could really get going I saw the look on Tom's face in the bathroom mirror and I shut up. There are times when I need to be reined in, and this was one of them.

I would like to be able to report that I was right about the baby, but I never did find out for sure; Wendy never told me. I did find out some truly horrifying details about their marriage, though, which surprised me, because I'd always thought they were happy. Of course, the only way to know what's been going on in somebody else's marriage is to talk to both parties while it is in the process of breaking up. There's a window there — a week, maybe two — when people will tell you everything. In fact, I think the reason people think married sex is so bad is because the only married sex they ever really hear about in any detail is from their friends whose marriages are breaking up, and the sex they describe is invariably awful.

"It just shouldn't take that much work for a person to have an orgasm," Darren said to Tom and me two days after Wendy finally left him. He was over at our apartment, getting drunk. "It was like trying to build a nuclear bomb," said Darren. "I'd be down there, trying to cross the yellow wire with the red wire, fiddling with the trigger mechanism, trying to remember exactly how I did it the last time it went off, and then, approximately forty percent of the time, success."

"It got to the point where I'd rather read a book," Wendy said to me over lunch later that week. "And it didn't have to be a good book."

"I don't even *like* big boobs," said Darren.

"I kept trying to convince myself, sex isn't everything," said Wendy.

"I miss her," Darren said, drunkenly. "I love her."

"I don't think I ever loved him," Wendy said, stabbing her salad with her fork.

"What do you mean, you never loved him," I said to Wendy. "You married him. You must have loved him."

"Now that I think about it," said Wendy, "I don't think I did."

"Maybe you just don't love him anymore," I said. "Maybe you loved him then, but at some point you stopped."

"No," Wendy said. "The night before we got married, I remember thinking to myself, I don't love this man."

"That's what you thought?" I said.

Wendy nodded. "Only it was too late. And then we were married, and it was *really* too late. And then one day my secretary walked into my office and told me she was getting a divorce, boom, one minute she was married and the next minute she was free, and while she stood there, sobbing uncontrollably, asking for extra personal days, it was like the clouds parted and everything became clear."

I went home that night and told Tom about my lunch with Wendy. He sat at the kitchen counter leafing through *Scientific American* while I made lemon chicken and floated theories at him. Maybe Wendy's pregnancy brought up memories of her mother abandoning her as a child, I said to him, and rather than face those feelings she decided to have an abortion, and rather than face that she decided to leave Darren.

"I don't get it," said Tom. "Do you still think it wasn't Darren's baby?"

"I'm not sure anymore," I said. "But it doesn't really matter whose baby it was. Even if it was Darren's baby, I'm still pretty sure there's somebody else."

"You always think there's somebody else," Tom said.

"I know I do," I said, "but that's not why I'm saying this."

"Why are you saying it?"

"Because Wendy is much too happy for there not to be somebody else."

"Maybe it's like pulling out a tooth," said Tom. "Maybe that's why she's happy."

I considered that for a moment. "It might not be an actual affair. It could just be the *idea* of somebody else."

"There's always the idea of somebody else," said Tom.

"No there isn't," I said.

"Yes there is," said Tom.

"There isn't for me," I said. "Why? Do you have the idea of somebody else?"

Tom just looked at me.

"It's fine if you do," I said. "I'd just like to know."

"Don't you think it's a little unrealistic to think that you, Alison Hopkins, so completely incorporate all the qualities of every woman in the entire world that I would never so much as entertain the *idea* of somebody else?" said Tom.

I didn't say anything.

"It's not having the idea that's the problem," Tom said. "Acting on the idea is the problem."

"Tell me one thing," I said, pounding the chicken with a meat tenderizer. "Are we talking about Kate Pearce?"

Tom sighed a big sigh.

"Just say yes or no."

"Alison."

"Because if she's the idea, we have a problem."

"We don't have a problem," said Tom.

"Good."

I almost feel proud of myself, remembering moments like that. At least I wasn't a total fool. At least I wasn't completely in the dark. Of course, later, after Tom left, Bonnie's husband Larry asked me if there had been any clues. I told him that there weren't any, but that was a lie; the apartment was full of them. I found them all eventually, and each one made me more angry than the last, angry that I hadn't snooped earlier, before Tom left, so I could have greeted him at the front door one day with a handful of credit card bills with incriminating charges and demanded an explanation. That would have been horrible, don't get me wrong, but at least I would have felt smart. Not that feeling smart would have made up for being betrayed and deceived and abandoned, but it would have been better than nothing.

That's one of the worst things about infidelity: how stupid it makes you feel. When Nina Peeble and I went out to lunch, she kept saying to me, "You must have known. A part of you must have known." And I can honestly say that I didn't. *I didn't know.* It's not a matter of looking the other way, it's a matter of not seeing anything at all. You're in the dailiness of the relationship, you're talking about work and life while you brush your teeth next to another person, and it simply doesn't occur to you that this other person who is involved in all that dailiness with you has an entirely separate life you don't know anything about. It just doesn't seem possible. Wouldn't it drive a person crazy? Wouldn't it make you out of your mind? Even now, knowing what I know, I still find it almost impossible to believe. In fact, sometimes I wish I had cheated on somebody just so I could understand the psychology of it, but the truth is I can't even imagine it. I can't imagine living with the guilt for sure, but the real problem for me would be keeping the secret. I'm no good with secrets. Six years ago, I was walking along South Street, and I was approached by a little old man who was wearing a turban. He told me how old I would be when I died (ninety-five), and that I would die in my sleep of a heart attack, and that I shouldn't get my hair cut or my nails clipped on Tuesdays, that, in fact, Tuesdays were extremely unlucky for me, and a big wave of good luck was about to come to me, and in the course of all this, which involved writing things down on little pieces of yellow paper and crumpling them up and putting them into my fist, he took eighty of my dollars, in increments of twenty, and gave me a small orange bead. "You give your good luck away by talking," he said to me when he was finished. "Do not give away your luck. Do not tell anybody what happened today." I felt like I was going to explode. Not tell anybody? I'd never done anything in my life and not told *somebody*. But for some reason this time I didn't, and for six years I kept that small Indian con man's confidence, and the secret burned inside me, burned and burned, and here I see I've gone and blown it.

Even without the secret part, though, the truth is I still can't imagine cheating on somebody. Do I secretly think this makes me a good person? I'm afraid I do. Do I occasionally find myself awash in a warm bath of my own moral superiority? You bet. But there is another way of looking at it. Maybe the only reason I haven't been a worse person is because I've been afraid to be one. If fear is what keeps you good, if fear is what keeps you out of trouble, then it shouldn't really count, right? You're just a fearful, timid person living a small, safe life, and the thought that that kind of existence takes some sort of moral courage is just, well, poppycock.

Sixteen

As upset as I had been about the whole thing between Tom and Kate, you should probably know that, all along, I'd been entirely prepared to take him back. That there was never any doubt in my mind that I would is actually quite odd, because I'd always thought of myself as a one-strike-and-you're-out sort of woman. I had, on more than one occasion, articulated this position to Tom. What I would say was that I knew that there were women who were capable of forgiving sexual misconduct, women who would be content to throw a dinner plate at the cheater's head and then try again, but I was not one of them. And I believed it, too. I honestly did. It's almost as if I had built an entire part of my personality around the idea that I was the kind of woman who would not stand for this sort of thing, only now, here I was, finally faced with the reality, standing it. I felt like I needed to completely reevaluate myself.

Which is not to say that I planned to make it easy for him. Quite the contrary, in fact. So, at the end of the little scene on the front stoop, I sent Tom away. I went inside and called up Cordelia and Bonnie, and the three of us met for lunch.

"I told him I needed some time to think about it," I said to them after we sat down.

"Which you do," said Cordelia.

"And I told him I had sex with somebody, too. After he was gone."

"You told him that?" said Bonnie.

"Yes," I said.

"What did he say?" said Bonnie.

"Nothing, really," I said. "He asked if he could move back in."

"He's out of his mind if he thinks he's moving back in," said Bonnie.

"I know," I said. "That's what I said."

"Good," said Bonnie.

"Then he asked if there was anything he could do, anything at all, and I said, 'Well, I suppose you could try to win me back.'"

Bonnie smoothed her yellow sweater over her enormous pregnant belly and nodded her head approvingly.

"Is that what you want?" said Cordelia.

"I don't know what I want," I said.

Cordelia looked at me.

"I don't think what I want matters," I said.

"Of course it matters," said Cordelia.

"I want for none of this to have happened," I said.

"Okay," said Cordelia. "What do you want that can be achieved while keeping the laws of space and time intact?"

"I don't know," I said. I thought about it for a moment. "It's like this broken, ruined thing, and no matter how much work we do to fix it, it will never be as good as what we had before."

"It's going to be better than what you had," said Bonnie. "He was cheating on you."

"It might be better than what I had," I said, "but it's not going to be better than what I thought I had."

And that was one of the things that made me so irritated. I was starting to come to terms with the fact that I'd been living in a dream, that what I'd thought was going on between Tom and me and what actually was going on were two wildly different things, but I couldn't quite accept that this realignment with reality was such a good thing. I liked the dream. I liked the fantasy. I have a problem with reality under the best of circumstances, and these were not the best of circumstances.

"At least you got to sleep with somebody else while he was gone," Cordelia said to me.

"Don't you sort of regret that now?" said Bonnie.

"Why would I regret it?" I said.

"Because if you get back together with Tom, for the rest of your life you're going to have a movie in your head starring this other guy."

"Hey, I like that movie," I said. "I would buy tickets to see that movie."

Cordelia excused herself to go to the restroom. She took a few steps away from the table, and then she turned right around and came back. She stood beside the table and looked down at me.

"Just don't confuse Tom coming back with winning," said Cordelia.

"What do you mean?" I said.

"I made that mistake with Jonathan," said Cordelia. "He would come back to me, with his tail between his legs, and I'd feel like I won, like I beat the other woman in some sort of contest, when really what had happened was, I'd just gotten back together with a total jackass." Then she walked off.

Bonnie reached past her belly and across the table and squeezed one of my hands.

"It's going to be okay," Bonnie said. "You know that, don't you?"

I shrugged my shoulders.

"Promise me one thing," Bonnie said.

"What?"

"Promise me you'll take it slow."

"Of course," I said. "Slow. Obviously."

Tom came over that night to pick up his clubs for an early-morning golf game; eight minutes later we were in bed. I know it was eight minutes exactly because of the digital clocks on the cable boxes, which are synchronized. When the doorbell rang, the cable box in the living room said 9:13, and then, while I was kneeling on the duvet, peeling off my turtleneck, I happened to glance at the cable box on top of the dresser, which glowed 9:21.

So we had sex. And I was conscious of many things while Tom and I were having sex that first time back, but the main thing I was conscious of was whether or not we were doing everything the way we used to, and if not, just what exactly had changed. I realize that sounds bad, but I couldn't help myself. I blame it on Matt, or, more specifically, I blame it on a story Matt tells which deals with this subject. This is the story. When Matt was a junior in college, his girlfriend Daisy went to Puerto Rico with her girlfriends for spring break. Now, Matt and Daisy had started out as one of those weird freshman-dorm couples that reach an almost matrimonial level of intensity and exclusivity by the third week of college and then just keep on keeping on, cooking ramen noodles together and wearing one another's jeans. So, Daisy comes back from her week in Puerto Rico. She and Matt climb into bed. Midway through the encounter, she flips him over onto his stomach and — and I'm sorry, but there is truly no polite way to describe this, so I will settle for clinical accuracy — she begins to stimulate his anus with her tongue. And, to hear Matt describe it, somewhere in the back of his head, a little bell went off. Which he elected to ignore. He did not ask Daisy how she happened to come up with this daring new trick. He did not immediately call a stop to the proceedings and grill her on just what exactly had gone on in Puerto Rico. He just lay there, really. (You're wondering how I know this. Well, men can be terribly indiscreet if you press them to be, and I always press them to be.)

After we were finished, Tom said a few of the things a person says in that situation, and then he fell asleep. I lay awake, staring up at the ceiling. There had been no new tricks. Oh well, I remember thinking. That's done, then. Maybe Kate Pearce was The Woman Tom Needed To Sleep With To Realize How Much He Loved Me. It looks like I'm stopping at three. Then, this: I wondered if I could marry a man who had cheated on me. I wondered if it would be smart. Probably not, I decided. I wondered if the fact that it wasn't smart would stop me. Probably not.

A lot has been said on the subject of women in their thirties who want to get married, and I'm not at all sure that I can add anything new. Still, I consider myself something of an expert in the field, if only because the anxiety that most unattached women start to feel around, say, their twenty-ninth birthday, kicked in for me at age thirteen. And then it began to build. Not getting married had been my worst fear for so long that I almost think I shouldn't be held responsible for my behavior regarding the subject.

There is a certain sort of pity and disdain that is reserved for single women in the evangelical subculture that the dominant culture — even with the help of its periodic *Time* magazine cover stories about escalating infertility rates and six-single-women-for-every-available-man statistics and misogynistic crap about forty-year-old spinsters and plane crashes — can never hope to equal. Because when an evangelical woman doesn't manage to find a husband, it is viewed as an unmitigated tragedy. For an ordinary single woman, the tragedy appears, to outsiders at least, to be mitigated. It is mitigated by the fact that she's meeting new men, she's taking fun trips, she's kissing in dark hallways at parties, she's waking up with promising strangers, she's eating takeout in bed with old boyfriends after sexual encounters that begin with the phrase "This is not a good idea." Her life might be sad and lonely and scary at times, but at least it's interesting. Not so, the nice Christian girl's. She is, at root, a dutiful handmaiden to the patriarchy, with oversize muffin pans in her cupboard and dried flowers arranged on her mantelpiece, always cheerful, always upbeat, always well-groomed and well-spoken and well-behaved. All of this while hoping against hope to meet a man who believes exactly the right thing in exactly the right way and who also happens to be intelligent and kind and funny and handsome and I forget the other twelve. I mean, it's hard enough to find *anybody* you might want to spend your life with, but if you are more or less forced to narrow the field down to the six weird bachelors milling around outside the sanctuary on Sunday morning — one of whom looks a little too intentionally like Jesus — things start to feel a little hopeless. And I think it's no accident, really, that I finally decided to have sex when I was twenty-five, because a part of me decided that if God was going to force me to be a freak, then at least I was going to have sex.

I keep thinking I have said all I have to say on this subject, that I have thoroughly bludgeoned the life out of it, but apparently I haven't. I see also that I have once again veered dangerously close to strident — a quality I have been informed is exceedingly unattractive on me — but I can't seem to help that either. Oh, well. A few months before all this happened, I bumped into an old family friend who has a daughter who is my age. This woman's daughter and I went to church together, and we sang in the choir together, and we went to camp together, and even though we haven't spoken in years, I consider her a friend. This person told me, in a very casual way, on a street corner while we were waiting for the light to change in fact, that her daughter always says she hopes Jesus won't come back before she gets married, because she doesn't want to miss her chance to have sex. Then she laughed. Now, this raises all sorts of questions — not the least of which is why this woman felt the need to tell me that her thirty-two-year-old daughter was still a virgin — but the reason I bring it up is because, the entire time I was growing up, I felt exactly the same way. I needed to get married as soon as possible, for the simple reason that I didn't want Jesus to come back before I had sex, and I wasn't allowed to have sex before I got married, so I needed to get married before Jesus returned, which everyone knew could happen at any moment. *Like a thief in the night.* Now, this perfectly captures certain suspicions I had about sex — namely, that it was of utmost importance and something I did not want to miss out on — as well as my quite matter-of-fact belief that before too long, Jesus Christ was going to come out of the eastern sky in a blaze of glory, sword in hand, and usher in Armageddon. (Precisely what happens next varies, depending upon one's theology, but the one thing everyone seems to agree upon is that there will be no sex involved.)

It's a miracle, really, that I am capable of anything even remotely normal after all that. When you start out where I started — waiting for Jesus to return to earth to herald the end of time — and end up where I was at this point in the story (lying in bed after having had sex with your live-in boyfriend after he has spent the past five months screwing around on you behind your back), you find yourself in a tricky position, which is that you cannot trust your instincts. Forget trusting them — you can't even find them. You have no idea where they are. Even now, I'm not sure what a woman with healthy instincts would have done in my situation. I'm always fascinated by women who seem to know things in their bones, women who possess that earthy, feminine wisdom that flies in the face of logic and reason and rational thought. Any instincts I might have had were wrung out of me a long time ago, and I'm afraid I'm left with a system in which everything has gone a little haywire.

Seventeen

I WOKE UP THE FOLLOWING MORNING WITH A START. I'D HAD A nightmare. I looked over and saw Tom asleep beside me, and seeing him there was such a shock that I almost forgot the dream entirely, but as I lay still, it slowly came back to me.

When Tom woke up, I told him about the dream. Then I began to interpret it — using Jungian principles I'd picked up from Janis Finkle — but Tom interrupted me before I could really get going.

"You're every person in the dream," said Tom.

"Parts of me, yes," I said.

"You're a young black man," he said. "And an old woman, and a baby that is really just an enormous head."

"And I'm the boat and I'm the water," I said. "And I will have achieved mental health when I can accept the fact that I'm the shark, too."

Tom gave me a look.

"What?" I said.

"I don't know," said Tom.

He rolled out of bed and headed for the bathroom.

"What?" I said again.

"Maybe a person shouldn't be their own hobby," Tom called from the bathroom.

"What is that supposed to mean?" I called back.

Tom didn't answer. I got out of bed and walked over to the bathroom. I leaned against the doorjamb and watched as he brushed his teeth.

"I'm my own hobby," I finally said.

Tom cocked his head at me in the mirror.

"I don't read self-help books," I pointed out.

"*Anymore*," Tom said. He spat. "You don't read self-help books *anymore*. But it's all in there." He tapped on my temple with his forefinger.

"Don't you think it's a little early in the game for you to be insulting me?"

"I didn't mean it as an insult," said Tom. "I meant it as an observation."

I raised an eyebrow at him but decided to let it go. "Tell me one of your dreams," I said.

"We've been through this before," said Tom.

"Just a teeny tiny one."

"I don't have dreams," he said.

"Everybody has dreams."

"I don't remember my dreams," said Tom. "And even if I did,

it wouldn't matter, because I'd wake up and I'd say to myself, it was just a dream."

This brings me to something about Tom that I'm not sure I've quite adequately conveyed: the fact that he is completely non-neurotic. I am fascinated by non-neurotic people, but not for any healthy reason, not because I want to try to become more like them. I have but one goal: to make them as crazy as I am. I think that happens a lot. I think that when a neurotic person gets involved with a non-neurotic person, the neurotic one inevitably believes that the normal one is repressing all of their inner turmoil and then, quite deliberately, sets about letting it loose. And I tried with Tom. Believe me, I tried. Now that I think about it, that's just about the only positive thing I can say about Tom's affair with Kate Pearce. It gave the man some much-needed subtext. It gave him underbelly. All along I'd been thinking that Tom was just going about his life, going to work and reading his science magazines and playing golf and trying not to get married to me, and here it turned out that wasn't true. Here there was suddenly all this new stuff to pick apart.

Of course, it's possible that I'm not being entirely fair to Tom. It's possible that he was deeper and more complicated than he appeared, and I just missed it, like I apparently missed so many other things that were going on between us. One problem was that I could never figure out what he was thinking. I never really knew what he was feeling either, but the thinking part is what gets me, because it seems so basic. And if I'm completely honest with myself, I suppose the truth is that Tom was always a little bit fuzzy to me. It's not that he was constantly surprising me, showing new and unexpected sides of himself; it's more that he was sort of a blank. That sounds much worse than I mean it to sound, but I can't think of how else to put it. When Tom and I first started dating, I told my sister Meredith all about him over the phone. A few months later, she flew into town on business, and the three of us went out to dinner. When Tom excused himself to go to the bathroom, I turned to Meredith and said, well? He seems nice, she said. I nodded my head for more. He's not quite what I pictured, she said. I pressed her to elaborate, and she finally said, well, he's really nothing like you described him. Now, my sister can get like that sometimes, but still. *Nothing* like I described him? How was that possible? I haven't thought about that for years, but now that I do, it makes me wonder.

There's something else I haven't thought about in a long time, but now that I'm thinking it I suppose I ought to tell you. It has to do with Kate Pearce. I suppose you could call it the history of Kate Pearce as she pertained to my relationship with Tom. It started, as these things so often do, with a photograph.

A few weeks after Tom and I first started dating, I was over at his apartment, looking through his photo album. Tom has a man's photo album. It completely skips over vast periods of his life, and there are still a lot of empty pages in the back. It gives the impression that he's going to go on through his life, slowly sticking in random pictures that his friends send him in the mail, and then, when he gets to the final page, he'll die.

"Who's she?" I said to Tom when I got to the picture.

"That's Kate."

"She's beautiful," I said. She was, too. She had big brown eyes and long brown hair and a sort of little-girl frailty that made me want to puke.

"How long were you guys together?" I said.

"Three years," said Tom.

"That's a long time."

"It was college."

"Three years in college is a very long time," I said. "What's she doing now?"

"I don't know. I haven't spoken to her in ten years."

"Why not?" I said.

"Things ended badly," he said.

"Badly how?"

"I don't feel like talking about it right now," he said.

I kept flipping through the album. Later that evening, though, I brought things around to the subject of Kate again, and Tom and I had the following exchange:

"So, do you still have feelings for her?" I said.

"I think it would be strange if I didn't have any feelings for her," said Tom.

"Are you still in love with her?" I said.

"I don't even know what that means," he said.

Of course I should have immediately said, "What do you mean you don't know what that *means*?" I should have at least tried to pin him down on what part he didn't understand. But this was early on in our relationship, maybe four weeks in, and you don't say things like that at the beginning of a relationship.

I'm not even sure you say them in the middle of one. Maybe you could get away with it at the end, I don't know, but if you're anything like me you just file away the information somewhere in the back of your brain and then do your best to forget that it's there. And I had pretty much forgotten about it — Kate Pearce was nothing more to me than a name, a name that had elicited a wistful, faraway look in my new boyfriend's eyes a long time ago, a look that I decided to interpret as his longing for youth, for freedom, for college girls swinging lacrosse sticks across impossibly green fields — for the past *in general* rather than for her *in particular.*

Two years later. A Saturday. Tom and I were buying groceries at the little place on Pine Street. They were his groceries; I was just along for the ride. We got up to the register and Tom swiped his card in the card swiper. He punched in his secret code. It was 5-2-8-3. "Did you pick your secret code or did the bank give it to you?" I said, in a completely innocent, making-conversation-while-in-line-at-the-grocery-store kind of way. "I picked it," Tom said, and then he got a strange look on his face. That's all it was, just a strange look, but at that moment I knew. I *knew.*

"Oh my God," I said.

Tom took his groceries and walked out of the store. I followed him.

"I can't believe this," I said.

"Alison," he said. "Please don't make a big deal out of this."

"I'm not making it a big deal," I said.

"I've had it since college. It doesn't mean anything," he said.

"It spells Kate," I said. "It means Kate."

"It's just a pattern to me now."

"That's not the point," I said.

"What is the point?" said Tom.

Well, I knew what the point was. I knew perfectly well what the point was. The point was that Tom's punching in Kate's name every time he visited the bank machine was representative of a certain sort of devotion, a certain quality of love that I'd spent the past two years thinking he was incapable of, and here it turned out he was capable of it, only, it would seem, not for me. That was the point. But I wasn't going to tell Tom that. No sir-ee. Because I didn't want him to realize that that was the point. Tom loved me. I knew he loved me. He loved me, but he had his issues. He had his baggage. Well, we all have issues, right? We all have baggage. And you must keep in mind that Kate Pearce was, at the point when this disturbing little episode took place, a relatively abstract problem. The man hadn't spoken to her in over *ten years*. And I had long given up on the idea of being somebody's first, last, and only. You have to give that up, it seems to me, unless you marry your high school sweetheart, and there is nothing in the world more boring than a person who is married to their high school sweetheart.

"I don't know what the point is," I said to Tom. I started to cry. "It just makes me feel bad."

Tom changed his secret code to my birthday, and our relationship resumed its course.

ॐ

Perhaps you're wondering whether or
Tom and Kate Pearce was in fact true love.
crossed my mind on more than one occasion. I m
after they broke up, the man was still punching her n
the bank machine every time he needed cash. It is, I suppose,
modern-day equivalent of carving somebody's initials over and
over again into the bark of oak trees. And I like to think that I'm
not the kind of person who would stand in the way of true love,
even if it meant that the person I was involved with ended up in
true love with somebody else. Tom and I only had one real conversation about Kate after he came back, only one conversation
that had any meat on it, and it dealt with precisely this subject. I
sat him down on the couch one night that first week back and I
said to him, you should think about this. Because maybe you
will regret it. Maybe you love her, maybe you need her, maybe
she is who you've wanted all along. And Tom assured me, no. It
wasn't about love, he said. It wasn't about Kate. Come to think
of it, he said it wasn't even about sex. Then what was it about?
you're wondering. He didn't really say. I do remember that he
took my hand in his, and he kissed it several times. He said that
he loved me. I said I loved him back. We sat in silence for a moment, breathing.

"Are we through now?" said Tom.

"Sure," I said. "Sure."

He let go of my hand and turned on the TV.

THE FOLLOWING WEEKEND, ON SATURDAY, I WENT BACK TO the office to clean out my desk. I was trying to avoid people, and at first it looked like I'd succeeded, too, but I hadn't. Because in walked Henry. He walked in and, without a word, flopped down on the beat-up couch that Matt had found propped up against the curb a few blocks from the office.

"That couch used to have fleas," I finally said.

"So did I," said Henry.

I fished my arm way back into my top drawer and pulled out an old checkbook from Mellon Bank. I started ripping up the checks and throwing them into the garbage can.

"When?" I said.

"What?"

"When did you have fleas?"

"Actually, I've never had fleas," said Henry. "I was just trying to make conversation."

He stretched out on the couch. "In college, this guy I knew named Judd had a couch with crabs."

I didn't respond.

"And, once, I found a tick on my uncle," he said.

I ripped up the last check. Then I looked over at Henry.

"You don't find this at all strange?" I said.

"Not really, no."

"It should be strange," I said. "You should find this strange."

"I think you're a little strange," Henry said, with a smile.

"I'm the normal one here, Henry," I said. "And I'm rarely the normal one."

I pulled out the bottom drawer of my desk and upended it into the garbage can. A few of my old clips fell to the linoleum, and I bent down to pick them up.

"Do you always analyze things while you're in the middle of them?" said Henry.

"We're not in the middle of anything anymore," I said. "And yes, I do."

"I'm sorry about your job," said Henry.

"That is not the thing to which I am referring."

"The Reading Terminal thing."

"Yes," I said.

"I see."

"I especially liked the part where you squeezed my shoulder," I said.

"Did I do that?"

I nodded. "I've never had someone break up with me and squeeze my shoulder before."

"I didn't break up with you," said Henry. "I told you I didn't think I could handle you. There's a difference."

"There is?"

"There is," said Henry. "And while this might be a technicality, there was nothing officially defined to break up."

"So, what, you were just telling me that so I wouldn't wait around for the next thirty years, hoping for you to show up on my doorstep and have sex with me again?"

"Jumping every time your phone rings."

"With my legs perpetually shaved."

"Yes," said Henry. He smiled at me. "I was trying to spare you that."

"That was very kind of you," I said.

"Thank you."

"And I take back everything I said."

"You didn't say anything," said Henry.

"I take back everything I said about you in my head," I said. "During my hating you period."

I walked over to the bookshelf and began to go through the books. I could feel Henry's eyes on me.

"When I was in sixth grade, I used to go to the roller rink every Saturday afternoon," I said. "One day, I noticed that this really cute boy kept staring at me. He would skate past me, and stare at me, and then skate past me again, and stare at me some more, and I was getting more and more excited each time it happened. Then finally, he skated right up to me and he fell in step beside me and he said" — and here I paused, as I always do when I recount this particular anecdote — "'Are you a boy or a girl?'"

Henry laughed. "That did not happen."

"It did. And then, when my mom came to pick me up, I started crying, and I told her what happened, and do you know what she told me?"

He shook his head no.

"She said, 'He just said that because your skates are black.' We didn't have much money, and I had hand-me-down skates from my cousin, and they happened to be black."

"That's a good mother," said Henry.

"Yes."

"And that's a good story."

"I know it is," I said. "But I'm telling it to you for a reason, and the reason is, I'm hereby officially putting you in that category."

"What category?"

"The skate-by guy."

I put the last few books into the box and told Henry I was leaving. He got up off the couch and put the box of my stuff under his arm and carried it into the hallway.

"Do you know what's going to happen to you, Henry?" I said.

"What?"

I looked up at him. "You're going to end up with a woman who can handle this sort of thing."

I pulled an old publicity photo of Woody Allen off the wall and switched off the light. When we got downstairs, I took my box from Henry and thanked him for carrying it. We stood together in front of the building. The *Philadelphia Times* banner flapped lazily in the breeze.

Henry caught my gaze and then quite pointedly didn't look away. I never know how to handle that move — the meaningful stare — and this time was no different. I started smiling, and then Henry started smiling, and then I started to laugh. I couldn't help myself. I looked down at the sidewalk.

"I'd like to ask you one last question," I said.

"This is the last question?" said Henry.

"Well, I'm going to my house, and you're going to your house, and I'm not working for you anymore, so yes, it's the last question. And I'd like you to be completely honest, even if you think it might hurt my feelings."

"Fire away."

I tried to think of the best way to put it. "What kind of sex would you say we were having, back when we were having it?"

"What do you mean?" said Henry.

"I mean, good, bad, average. What kind of sex was it?"

Henry looked up at the sky, like he was searching the clouds for the right word.

"Outstanding," said Henry.

"I thought so," I said.

I hailed a cab and headed home.

I sat in the cab with the box of my stuff on the seat next to me. I felt good. Henry had turned out to be a pleasant diversion. Like a tantalizing confection you eat someplace foreign you know you'll never return to. Certain people come into your life, and you can't hold on to them; you simply take what they have to offer and try to give them something in return. Maybe this is growth, I thought. Not clinging so hard to things. Even my job. I could feel myself letting go of that, too, which was good, since I didn't have it any longer. I would find another job. And now Tom was home and everything was falling back into place. I gazed out the window. I smiled a smug smile. *Outstanding*.

I glanced down at the box beside me. My desk calendar was on top, fluttering in the wind streaming in from the driver's open window. How long had it been since the dinner party? I wondered. I reached over and flipped back through the pages. Just over three weeks. I was amazed. It felt like two years had gone by. I started slowly turning the pages, running the events of the past weeks through my mind. My brain flashed on a pornographic moment with Henry. I blushed, and closed my eyes.

Then I opened them. I blinked hard. I grabbed my calendar and started flipping back through the pages. Back to the dinner party. I flipped further back. Finally I saw it, in the lower right-hand corner of one of the pages.

A small x.

I looked at the date on the page with the x. I counted weeks on fingers. Five fingers. Five weeks!

A wave of nausea came over me, and I felt clammy and panicky and terrified. I grabbed the armrest to steady myself. Take a breath, I commanded myself. This doesn't mean anything. This could be nothing. I kept trying to calm myself with a rational inner dialog, but down below there was another voice, a much more authoritative one, which was telling me in no uncertain terms that I was pregnant.

"Hey lady," said the cabdriver.

I looked up. The taxi was in front of my building. Tom was upstairs, I knew, watching a golf tournament on TV. Completely oblivious. Like nothing at all monumental was going on inside my womb.

"Um, there's a second stop. Nothing's happening at this stop. I just wanted to drive by," I couldn't stop babbling. "I thought someone might, but now it turns out they're not . . ."

"Whatever," said the cabbie, and I gave him the new address.

I sat back and started furiously flipping through the calendar, trying to remember things I hadn't thought about since eighth grade health class. Like when ovulation took place. Was it twelve days after your last period stopped? Or did you count based on when your last period *started*? Sixteen days or so? I realized I had no idea. After that, how many days was the egg in play? Three, maybe? Five? I started to sweat. I pictured my insides as a big cesspool filled with sperm that had managed to bypass the various defenses employed against them, sperm lurking around for days, weeks even, making their own ecosystem, my womb a giant snow globe of foreign genetic material, a single unsuspecting egg floating down like a balloon in a stadium filled with confetti. I tried to remember exactly when I'd had sex. I folded down the corners of various pages. *Four times on two separate occasions.* Should a second time that took place after midnight count for the following day? I wondered. Because that's a lot of folded pages. I sat there, staring at my dog-eared calendar, as a truly horrifying realization started to sink in.

I didn't know whose baby it was.

I didn't know whose baby it was! It could have been Tom's, or it could have been Henry's! It was probably Henry's, but it might have been Tom's! And they didn't even look alike! Tom had blond hair and Henry had brown! I started to hyperventilate. I tried to remember what Tom had said about our children's eyes. Something about how he knew what color they would be. Well, Tom had blue eyes and Henry's were brown! I was doomed!

The taxi turned onto Cordelia's street and pulled up in front of her building. I thrust a crumpled twenty over the front seat, and while I was waiting for my change, I folded my arms across my chest and discreetly pressed my forearms against my breasts. Which were tender. Tender!

"Here you go," said the cabdriver. He handed me my change.

I headed into Cordelia's apartment building. I nodded to Enrique the doorman, and he waved me on through. I got into the elevator and pressed the button for the eleventh floor.

I stood alone inside the elevator. Shame settled over me like a mantle. When had I turned into a whore? I asked myself. What had happened? Where had I gone wrong? How had I come to the conclusion that any of this was acceptable behavior? I was living with a man I wasn't married to, and I'd slept with a guy I'd known for less than a week, on our first date. Which wasn't even really a date, come to think of it. The man had asked me to dinner in a stairwell. We'd split the check. I might as well have put an ad in the back of our paper and asked him to leave the cash on top of the dresser on his way out. I watched the numbers of the floors light up, one by one, and my eyes filled with tears. Well, Alison, I said to myself, you are reaping what you sowed. You sowed sluttish behavior, and now you are going to reap an unwanted child whose paternity is in no way certain.

The elevator doors opened. I walked down the long, poorly lit hallway and rang Cordelia's doorbell.

"What's wrong?" Cordelia said when she saw my face.

"I'm pregnant," I said, and I burst into tears.

Cordelia nodded her head calmly and let me in. I flung my coat over a chair and threw myself face-down onto her couch.

"I'm going to kill myself," I said.

"You took a test?" she said flatly.

"You know how Bonnie says every time she gets pregnant, she knows?" I said. "Well, I *know*."

Cordelia walked into her kitchenette and pulled a bottle of Absolut out of the freezer. She poured us each a big drink.

"Drink," she said.

I sat up and shook my head no. "The baby," I said.

Cordelia rolled her eyes at me.

"What?" I said.

"Do you know how many times we've had this conversation, Alison?"

"More than once."

"Many, many times more than once."

"And I'm never pregnant," I said.

"And you're *never* pregnant."

"Never."

"You're never pregnant. You work yourself up and you get hysterical and you never once have gotten pregnant."

This was the truth.

Now, without getting too explicit about my inner workings, this whole thing with me has always been a rather inexact science. I do not run like clockwork. I run in a manner designed to create the maximum number of niggling suspicions and false alarms and full-blown pregnancy scares. And perhaps you think that a normal person with a history like mine would exercise some caution when leaping to the kind of conclusions I leapt to in the back seat of the cab. Perhaps a normal person would. Not me. There is never a doubt in my mind. I'm always one hundred percent convinced. Now that I'm giving the matter some thought, it occurs to me that the whole system functions as my own personal penance for having sex. For while I have, on a conscious level, quite rationally decided that having sex with an individual to whom you are not married is okay so long as neither party is married to or otherwise entangled with anybody else, my subconscious is down there going *not so fast*. And so it starts lobbing up fears. And diligence of application of various prophylactic measures does not do anything to mitigate them. I trace this back to a girl in my youth group who got pregnant in high school and maintains — *to this day* — that she never actually, technically, entirely, had sex. So even multiple lines of defense mean nothing to my psyche.

"I know we've been through this before," I said, "but this time is different."

"Different how?"

"Because I don't know who the father is," I said, and I burst into tears again.

Cordelia put her hands on her hips. "Who are the candidates?"

"What do you mean who are the candidates?" I shrieked. "You know the candidates! Tom and Henry!"

There was a long pause.

"And they don't even look alike!" I said.

Cordelia cocked her head at me.

"They have different-colored eyes!" I said.

"That's your plan?"

"I don't have a plan!"

"Well, I do," said Cordelia. "Put your coat on."

"Where are we going?"

"To the drugstore."

I shook my head vigorously. "I can't," I said. "I can't take it."

"*I* can't take it," said Cordelia. "And I refuse to do this for one minute longer than absolutely necessary."

Cordelia and I took the elevator down and walked around the corner to the CVS. I plunked down the nineteen dollars for a test, the good one — nineteen dollars I could ill afford, now that I was unemployed. I trudged back to Cordelia's clutching the brown paper bag in a sweaty fist.

There is no need for me to draw this part out. I followed the directions on the box, I sat on the toilet for what seemed like an eternity with my eyes screwed closed, and then I opened them. Relief poured over me. There is no better feeling than this one. In fact, it strikes me that the only plus to this pregnancy hypochondria is that this feeling — the feeling of *not* being pregnant when you don't want to be — is so sublime. For a while, all of your regular problems seem so small and manageable in light of this new impossibly huge one, and then, with the simple act of peeing on a stick, the impossibly huge problem disappears.

"You know," Cordelia said to me, "we really have passed into the realm of behavior that ought to be evaluated by a mental health professional."

I nodded.

"This is not normal," she said.

I nodded again.

"Next time you think you are pregnant, remind yourself that you've never once gotten pregnant. You've been having sex for years, and you've never gotten pregnant. Not once."

She gave me a long hug.

"Cordelia?" I said into her neck.

"Yes?"

I pulled out of the hug and searched her face. "Do you think maybe I *can't* get pregnant?"

She hit me.

And I headed home.

೪

I have two theories about why it was that I took Tom back. No, I just thought of another one — so that makes three. Three theories. The first is that Tom leaving me for Kate Pearce was a blow to my narcissism, and his return fed into my ideas of my own incomparable self-worth. Janis Finkle was the first person to use the term *narcissist* in connection with me. She just casually lobbed it into one of our sessions, like it was something we had both acknowledged long ago, like it was a fact that had been written down in my file right next to the names of my siblings and the town I grew up in and my recurring dream about the boating accident. After our session, I went straight to Barnes & Noble and sat down on the mottled green carpet in the psychology section with the DSM-III open on my lap. I flipped to Narcissistic Personality Disorder. I read through the diagnostic criteria. I definitely had three of the indicators, and quite possibly four, while you needed five to be considered a clinical case. Which was cutting things a little close as far as I was concerned. When I saw Janis the next week, I really grilled her on the subject, to such an extent that I undoubtedly appeared to be obsessed with my own narcissism, like a snake that had developed a taste for its own tail. Anyhow, I don't believe I'm a primary narcissist — I am capable of acknowledging other people's feelings and seeing things from points of view other than my own — but I do have narcissistic tendencies, and when Tom told me he couldn't live without me, the narcissistic part of me perked right up. Of course he couldn't! Poor fellow! So. That's one. The second theory is a little more on the nose. Perhaps you have put together the following: that my father left when I was five, and — as I am on the record as having two fathers — he did not come back. So Tom's return was a reenactment of the central fantasy of my childhood, and on some level I was unable to resist it.

The third theory, as it turns out, is the only one I was aware of at the time. The third theory is that I loved Tom. And love makes you do crazy things. Of course, craziness also makes you do crazy things, but oh well. Tom was back. Things weren't what I'd thought they were, but I would survive. I'd never dreamed that I'd be able to stand something like this, but here it looked like I could. Just because I'd spent so many years coloring inside the lines, it wasn't fair for me to expect perfection. People make mistakes. Life isn't fair. People change.

When I got home, Tom was stretched out on the couch with his headphones on. His eyes were closed, and he was lying perfectly still, and for a moment it crossed my mind that he might be dead. He wasn't, of course; he was asleep. I shook the thought out of my head. I went into the kitchen and pulled a box of pasta from the cabinet and started to make dinner.

Nineteen

THE MOVIE *WHEN HARRY MET SALLY* DID A GRAVE DISSERVICE TO single people everywhere, by forcing them to look at every friend of the gender towards which they are drawn and wonder: is *that* who I'm going to end up with? And most of the time, this is not a hopeful, happy question, because if you *wanted* to end up with that person, you'd already be dating them. Imagine if somebody had told Meg Ryan on that drive from Chicago to New York that she would spend the next twelve years of her life single, punctuated by a handful of relationships that would be both unfulfilling and short lived, and then, finally, just as she is about to give up all hope, who will she be happy to see waiting for her at the end of the aisle? The idiot who just spit grape seeds on her window.

Which brings me to Matt. Matt, my dear friend Matt, who chose this particular moment in time to tell me that he was in love with me.

The whole thing came as something of a shock, of course, but it was not nearly as big of a shock as you might think. I did not know that Matt had feelings for me, I really had no earthly idea, but I do suffer from an affliction in which I believe that all of my male friends are secretly in love with me. I think that some of them are conscious of this fact and some of them aren't. There are women who have a variant of this affliction — women who go through life convinced every man they know wants to sleep with them — but that's not my problem. In fact, I think it's entirely possible that my male friends who are in love with me have little or no interest in sleeping with me, which is why these friendships manage, year after year, to continue apace. Anyhow, to have it finally happen, to have one of my friends proclaim his love for me, to have my intuition in this particular area verified pleased me the tiniest bit, but that bit was completely overshadowed by the rest of it, which was awful.

It happened at Doobies, and we had been drinking. Fine: we were drunk. Doobies is the kind of bar you go to to get drunk, and that's what we were doing. We each did a shot of tequila at the bar, and then we played a few games of darts. There was tequila involved with the dart games, too, and, due to a series of miscalculations in the number of points I was spotted, as well as my freakish ability to rise far above my natural gifts in competitive situations, Matt repeatedly lost. And drank.

After a while, a couple of off-duty waiters came in and wanted a game, so we moved to a booth. Matt went to the bar. He came back with a pitcher of Rolling Rock and a pack of Marlboros.

He took a cigarette out and lit it.

"What are you doing?" I said.

"What does it look like?" said Matt.

"You don't smoke," I said.

"I don't smoke *anymore,*" said Matt. "I quit on January 1, 1995."

I looked pointedly at the cigarette in his hand.

"It is one of my few real accomplishments in life," he said. "And the other day, as I was reflecting on that fact, I decided to reward myself with one month of unlimited cigarette smoking."

"You're out of your mind," I said.

"And then I'll quit again," said Matt. He took a long drag. "Although I do love these bad boys."

"Well, give me one too, then," I said.

Matt lit another cigarette and handed it to me.

"You know," said Matt, "sometimes I forget how sweet you used to be, but then I see you holding a cigarette like a twelve-year-old and it all comes back to me."

"What are you talking about?" I said. "I'm still sweet."

"No, you're not."

"Yes, I am."

He shook his head no.

I sat with this for a moment. "Well, I don't want to be sweet," I finally said. "Sweet, after a certain age, is just drippy."

"I don't know," said Matt. "Julie was sweet."

"Julie?"

"The nurse," he said.

"Right," I said. "The drippy one."

Matt got a wistful look on his face. "She was so into me. She was always doing things for me. Bringing me little presents. She would bake me these perfect miniature loaves of zucchini bread" — here he mimed the dimensions of the loaf, tenderly, thoughtfully, and I realized he was quite drunk — "and I thought there must be something wrong with her, to be that nice to me all the time. But the real problem was, I kept looking for something better."

"Why don't you call her?"

"She got married two years ago," he said. "She married a dentist. They live in Oregon."

"Maybe there's a lesson here," I said.

"The lesson of Julie," Matt said. He closed his eyes for a moment, and then he said, "The next time I find someone nice who can stand me, I'm just going to *hold on*."

He opened his eyes. He blinked at me.

"What?" I said.

"Nothing," he said.

"What is it?"

"Let's get married," said Matt. He stood up. His voice rose above the sound of the jukebox. "I'm serious. Marry me, Alison."

"Matt, sit down."

"If you won't marry me, at least come home with me," said Matt.

"Right."

"I don't want to be the guy who tries to get a woman into bed by promising how great it will be, but here I am, I'm doing it," he said. "It'll be great. I promise."

There were a couple of people sitting at the bar, and I could see them turning to watch.

"Matt, you're embarrassing me," I said in a low voice.

"I'm embarrassing you? I don't think so. If anyone ought to be embarrassed by this, it's me. But I don't care. And do you know why? Because I love you."

I leaned forward and hit him hard on the chest. I don't know why I did that, really, I'm not sure what the intended effect of the blow was, but whatever it was, it didn't work. Because Matt was merely emboldened.

"I am in love with you, Alison Hopkins," Matt said, truly loudly now, and I thumped him again.

One of the dart players called to the bartender, "Steven, get that gentleman another pitcher."

"Thank you, no," I called, and waved my hand in the direction of the bartender. "We don't need any more alcohol here."

I looked up at Matt. "Please sit down."

Matt sat back down. He reached across the table and grabbed both of my wrists in his hands. I could feel our pulses bouncing off each other.

"Look at me," he said.

I looked at him. His hair was sweaty around the edges, but his eyes were clear and bright and locked on mine.

"I love you, Alison," said Matt. "And I'm not just saying that because I'm drunk."

And with that, a feeling came over me that I can't for the life of me describe, but I knew he was telling me the truth. My heart dropped for him.

"Well, I'm probably saying it because I'm drunk," he continued, "but that doesn't mean I don't mean it. I do. I've loved you as long as I've known you."

I was stunned. I had no idea how to respond. In all those years of suspecting various friends of nursing secret feelings for me, I had never envisioned it going quite this far. Now that the actual moment was upon me, now that the declaration had been made, now that there was a man sitting before me with his heart in his hands, I just felt unbelievably sad.

"Oh, Matt," I finally said, somewhat lamely. "Matt."

He looked at my face. He let go of my wrists. "Say no more."

I felt horrible. It really was an awful moment. I was not remotely in love with Matt, you understand. And I knew that that was not going to change. And that simple truth — the utter impossibility of the situation as it was presently constituted — struck me as incredibly unfair. Unfair to whom? To Matt? Well, yes, obviously; but it felt bigger than that. It felt monumentally unfair, it felt cosmically unfair, it felt unfair to every last human being who ever walked upon the earth. Shouldn't love be simpler than this? Shouldn't this thing, this most fundamental of things, be easier and more predictable and less capricious and random and cruel? And if somewhere along the line I'd begun to confuse "falling in love" with "finding an appropriate man who is willing to let me work on my relationship with him," well, who could blame me? What exactly was the alternative? Well, I was looking at the alternative. And it was a very risky alternative.

The bartender set a fresh pitcher of beer in front of us and said, "Mazel tov."

Matt refilled his glass. He downed it dramatically, in a single breath, and then he set the empty glass back on the table with some force. I stood up to go to the bathroom. "Will you excuse me for a moment?"

"No, I won't," said Matt. "I'd like you to marinate in this awkwardness with me for a while."

I sat back down. I stared at my hands. They looked old. They looked too old for this.

"I really have to pee, Matt," I finally said. "And I'm not just saying that."

"Fine. Go. I'll just marinate by myself," said Matt. "You urinate, and I'll marinate."

When I came back from the bathroom, Matt was sitting quietly, shredding a napkin into long, thin strips.

"I've given some thought to what just happened here," said Matt.

"What did you come up with?" I said.

"My internal censor, which never works that well to begin with, was temporarily totally disabled," said Matt.

"I see."

"Due to the alcohol," he said.

"Yeah."

"The smoking makes me thirsty," he said. "And I forgot to eat dinner."

I nodded my head.

"We can just forget it, if you'd like," I said.

"That would be good," he said.

"Done," I said.

Somebody put "Love Hurts" on the jukebox.

"But I meant every word," Matt said, solemnly. "And you can't end up with Tom. He isn't worthy of you. He's worse than not worthy. He's a worthless god-awful prick." He stubbed out his cigarette. "And apparently the censoring mechanism is still disabled."

We sat in silence for a moment.

"We should probably go," I finally said.

"A good idea."

Matt walked me home. We walked through Fitler Square, past the turtle sculptures, and turned onto Delancey. When we got to my building, we stood on the sidewalk. The lights inside were out.

"It'll happen again, you know," said Matt.

"What are you talking about?"

"Tom. He'll do it again."

I dug around in my purse for my keys.

"It's a very fundamental thing, the way a person comports themselves in that particular department," said Matt.

"I don't know," I said.

"He'll do it again, and you'll have to decide if this is what you want."

⁊❧

The following Tuesday, I went to New York for an interview for a job at a magazine. I took the train up, had the interview, and on the way back, the train was very crowded. A woman who was about my age sat down in the seat beside me, and we started talk-ing. It turned out that she had gone to Wheaton College — the one in Illinois, the Christian one — with my sister Meredith. It turned out her father was the pastor of the church my friend Angie goes to down in Atlanta. It turned out, in short, that she was an evangelical Christian, and due to a small accretion of de-tails, she got the impression that I was much more of an evangel-ical Christian than I currently am. Now, when I find myself in such a situation these days, I do my best to honor my own expe-rience of things, and I try not to get involved in an inordinate amount of hypocrisy and personal misrepresentation; at the very least, I try to avoid telling any outright lies. Which isn't easy. This time, the conversation degenerated into me making the usual complaints about evangelicals. How they're self-righteous. How they're close-minded and judgmental and legalistic. The lack of intellectual rigor, the fear of art and culture and ideas, the near total disconnect from any sense of Christianity's historical roots. The bad hair, the bad clothes, the ugly churches, the cloy-ing singsong public prayer voice. And the smugness. Dear God, the smugness. "Forget all that," this woman said to me. "Forget *Christians.*" And she put her hand on my forearm, and she got one of those painfully sincere looks on her face, and she had a southern accent (and I think this is one of those things you can really only say if you have a southern accent), "Are you *in love* with Jesus?" And that kind of took me aback. Partially because people don't say things like that to me anymore. Partially because it made me think. And the truth is, I'm not in love with Jesus at the moment. That's not quite the right word for it. I'm haunted by Jesus, but I'm not really in love with him.

It would be wrong for me to suggest that I have lost my faith entirely, but I have lost a certain kind of faith, and I hope I haven't left you with the impression that losing it was anything less than a very big loss. I am left to deal with the remains of it all, to pick through it, to run from it, to rail against it, but I keep finding that even the remains of what I once had are powerful stuff. A certain sort of person would say this. A certain sort of person would say that what is really going on is that I'm running away from God. And you know what? That's exactly what it feels like. The truth is, my heart is restless, and I'd like some peace, and I'm starting to suspect that it is pride that keeps me where I am, but I can't seem to go back. Not yet anyway. Not just yet.

Twenty

NOTHING MUCH HAPPENED FOR A COUPLE OF WEEKS — WELL,
nothing much happened to me. Bonnie had her baby, so something fairly major happened to her. It was a girl, their first girl,
and they named her Grace. Cordelia and Naldo broke up. Matt
wrote me a sweet note, and I wrote him one back. Things with
Tom and me went more or less back to normal.

Then, late one Friday afternoon, I was in the bedroom straight-
ening up. I noticed a cash register receipt on the floor beside
Tom's dresser. I picked it up, and I was about to put it back on
top of his dresser when my glance happened to fall on the back
of it. I froze. There were two initials, followed by a telephone
number. I sat down on the foot of the bed and stared at the piece
of paper in my hands. I mean, who writes phone numbers after
initials? I'll tell you who. Somebody with something to hide.
Somebody who doesn't want the person they're living with to

know who it is that they're calling. Somebody who doesn't want the person they're living with to know the *gender* of the person that they're calling.

I looked at the clock. Tom would be home in less than an hour. We were driving out to Nina Peeble's house for one of her dinner parties. Nina was always throwing dinner parties, but this one was special. Bonnie and Larry were going to be there, and Cordelia, and Nina's husband Victor — everyone, in fact, who had been at the original dinner party, the one that ended so disastrously. Everybody had been instructed by Nina to act like nothing had happened, so we could get all the awkwardness out of the way in one fell swoop.

Which meant I had to move fast.

I walked into the kitchen. I put a pot of water on the stove, and I turned the heat on under it as high as it would go. Then I went into living room, over to Tom's desk. There was a stack of unopened mail on top of it, as I knew there would be. I flipped through the mail until I found what I was looking for. I did this all matter-of-factly, like I had taken a class in the subject, like I had seen some sort of instructional video. I went back into the kitchen with the mail and stared into the pot. Nothing. Nothing, for what seemed like an eternity. Then a few bubbles on the silver bottom. Slowly, slowly getting bigger. Finally, a nice, rolling boil.

I bent down and opened the drawer that held the rarely used cooking utensils. I searched for a pair of tongs. There was much clattering, but no tongs. The only thing remotely tong-like was a pair of old wooden salad spoons, but the hold wasn't tight enough; the envelope kept slipping out onto the counter. I took a breath. Maybe this is a sign. Maybe I should stop right now, take the pot off the stove, put the mail back on Tom's desk, because once I go down this road, I'm down this road. I looked at the clock on the microwave, and that's when I noticed the oven mitts. Oven mitts would work.

I held the envelope over the pot with one hand, and I used the other to test the seal. It didn't take long for the glue to lose its hold. Shouldn't our postal system be more secure that this? For a moment I had a very particular feeling, the feeling you get when you go through life knowing something — that peanut butter will get bubble gum out of hair, say, or that urine will ease the pain of a jellyfish sting — some bit of cultural wisdom you keep in your back pocket but never find occasion to use, and then, when you finally do, all you want to do is tell every last person you know how well it actually works.

I opened the envelope and unfolded Tom's cell phone bill. Every phone number was listed, along with the length and time of each call. I carefully compared the list of calls to the number on the back of the receipt. It wasn't there.

I kept staring at the list of numbers, trying to find a pattern, a clue, anything at all. An unfamiliar area code caught my eye. What's this? I ran my finger down the list of calls. One, two, three, four — seven. My heart started to pound. Seven calls to the mystery number. Always in the early evening. Always about twenty minutes long. Probably while he was walking home from the office.

I picked up the phone and dialed the number. It rang once. Then, again. I started to get nervous. Three times. Then, a woman's voice. "Hello?"

"Yes," I said. I hadn't thought up anything to say. "Hello."

"Alison?" the voice said.

Shit.

"To whom am I speaking," I said.

"It's Tracy, Alison. Tom's sister."

"Tracy. Right. Hi," I said. "Is, uh, Tom there?"

"No. Should he be?"

"I had the idea he would be."

"I didn't even know he was going to be in Boston," said Tracy.

"Yeah. I might have gotten it wrong."

"Have him call if he's in town," she said.

"Sure."

"Are you okay, Alison?"

"Yeah, I'm fine," I said.

"Okay," she said. "Well, good-bye, then."

"Good-bye."

I hung up the phone. My heart was pounding in my chest, and I started to pace around the kitchen. The water on the stove was still boiling. The steam billowed up, tempting me. I eyed Tom's American Express bill. I fingered the seal on the envelope. Maybe I should just take a little peek.

Stop it, Alison, I said to myself. This will not do. What is a relationship without trust? You have to forgive him. You have to trust him, or you'll go crazy.

I sat down at the kitchen table with my head in my hands. This is completely irrational, I told myself. It is totally unreasonable. And then it struck me: the problem was, it *was* rational. It was entirely reasonable. For the rest of my life, whenever I see a telephone number written in the margin of a date book, say, or on the back of a business card, I will feel it is my duty to investigate. To ask, at the very least. To make a seemingly innocent inquiry. I will hear a woman's name, and I will wonder. My head started to churn with the possibilities.

And what would I do if it happened again? Just what exactly was my plan? I suddenly saw that in a strange way I had been comforted by the fact that Tom and Kate had a history together, I'd been comforted by the belief that she was a truly unique obsession. Certain kinds of men get certain kinds of obsessions, and sometimes it's best to just ride it out. I never knew that I held to that particular theory, but apparently somewhere down deep, I did. I knew they weren't going to *end up* together. Even Tom knew that. That's one of the things he told me flat out. She's not the kind of woman I could marry is how he put it. Well? I mean, there could only be one Kate Pearce, right? Once she's out of the picture . . . right?

I opened the cabinet underneath the microwave and pulled out the white pages. I found the number I was looking for, and then I dialed.

"Is this Janis Finkle?" I said.

"Yes?"

"The Janis Finkle who used to work at Family Services?"

"Yes. Who's calling, please?"

"I used to be one of your patients. Clients. You were my therapist. My name is Alison Hopkins."

"Alison. Of course," Janis said. "How are you?"

"I'm fine. Not that fine, I guess. That's why I'm calling."

"What can I do for you?"

"I was wondering if there was something you figured out about me that maybe you could let me in on. You know, a secret."

"A secret," she said flatly, in that therapist way.

"I mean, I know you're not supposed to tell me what to do in therapy, but I thought you might have come up with a theory about me that you kept to yourself, that you were waiting for me to figure out on my own. Now that we're not doing it anymore, I wondered if maybe you could bend the rules."

"Why don't you tell me what it is that's upsetting you right now," said Janis.

So I did. I told her the whole story. I told her about Tom and Kate's affair, and what had happened at the dinner party, and how Tom finally came back with the mustard two weeks later. I told her about finding the phone number on the scrap of paper, and then steaming open the phone bill, and finding an entirely different number, and calling it, and how I was thinking now that maybe I should call the first number, that I should have called it in the first place, and I went on and on, and by the time I got through, I was sobbing into the phone expectantly, waiting for a moment of sympathy or compassion or understanding, and do you know what Janis Finkle said to me? She said, "How does it feel to not be in control?"

Fuck you, I remember thinking at the time. I'm not the one who cheated. I'm not the one who went out for the mustard and didn't come back. I didn't lie, I didn't break any promises, I didn't sneak around, I didn't diddle a little twinkie, I didn't ruin everything — I didn't do anything but paint the kitchen the perfect shade of yellow and buy baskets for the man's socks. *If I'd been in control, none of this would have happened!*

There was a period in my life when I spent a great deal of time arguing about whether or not it would be possible to throw a monkey out of a window. The window in question was on the twenty-third floor of one of the high-rise dorms at the University of Pennsylvania — I think I hardly need mention that this was in college — in an apartment-style dorm room just down the hall from mine, inhabited by four guys who always kept their front door propped open with a shoe. A lot of things got thrown out of that particular window, the most dramatic being a nineteen-inch television set, but there was no debate involved with that one, since there had never been any question about whether or not it would be *possible* to throw a television out the window. They could, and they did, and then they moved on to the monkey question and never quite got off it. Even now, it is possible to reignite this debate simply by assembling three or four individuals, so long as one of the people present is Lyle Brady. Lyle Brady was somewhat legendary at Penn. He was pre-vet, and he had grown up on a dairy farm in western Kentucky, and he was famous for his pickup line "You're so cool and pure, you're like a tall glass of milk." Lyle had the utmost confidence in the monkey's strength and reflexes and general will-to-live. Lyle, in fact, contended it would be categorically impossible to throw a monkey out of a window, and, even more essential for this sort of thing, never tired of debating the subject. There were a few agreed upon rules. The monkey in question was to be of the dimensions that his arms, when fully extended, could easily grasp both sides of the window frame, and he could not be physically impaired in any way; i.e., bound up, blindfolded, drugged, etc. But you could, for example, spin the monkey around and around and around and then hurl it out backwards — that was fair. Or you could, say, turn out all the lights. You could wait until the monkey fell asleep, or develop some sort of a high-speed catapult. You get the picture. Anyhow, it seemed to me that if you "made nice" with the monkey, if you held it facing you and cooed at it like a mother to a baby as you slowly made your way across the room to the open window, and then just chucked it, the monkey would be so surprised that it wouldn't have the wherewithal to grab the window frame and out it would go. To this day, I'm so confident that this particular strategy would work that I'd like to get my hands on an actual monkey and try it out. Not from the twenty-third floor, of course. Perhaps the second.

Go with me for a minute. One of the major disappointments of my adult life has been finding out just how little being smart has to do with love. I've always relied on my brains to get me through, I've always secretly believed that I had a leg up in life because I was, if not the smartest person in the room, at least the one that the smartest person in the room would pick to talk to, and I figured that that would make me good at love. But the truth, the truth that I'm just starting to see, is that being intelligent and being good at love are two entirely different things, and thinking that one thing will make you good at the other is like expecting a world-class juggler to be able to perform brain surgery. It strikes me, in fact, that I was so busy outsmarting Tom that I stopped really loving him. I was so busy trying to turn him from a date into a boyfriend into a fiancé into a husband that I stopped paying attention. I thought that took brains. I thought that took skill. I was so intent on pursuing a tactical advantage that I stopped doing anything else. On some level, I was just trying to chuck him out the window. And do you know what happens when you do that? Do you know what you've got on your hands? I'll tell you what you've got.

A dead monkey.

I finally figured out what I'd wanted from Tom all along. I wanted him to stay. I wanted him to stay *forever*.

Twenty-one

WHEN I GOT OFF THE PHONE WITH JANIS FINKLE, I WENT INTO the bathroom and jumped into the shower. I was angry. I was angry with Tom for writing a phone number after initials, I was angry at Janis for insinuating that I was controlling, and I was angry at myself for accidentally calling Tom's sister Tracy. I was preemptively angry at Tracy, because I knew she would report back to Tom about my phone call, and I was angry with myself because I couldn't for the life of me come up with a reasonable explanation for it. I was even kind of angry at Nina Peeble, for thinking that this dinner party was a good idea in the first place.

And I was mad at Tom, because he was late.

Nina and her husband Victor live about twenty-five minutes outside the city, in a huge house in Rosemont. When Tom came home, he changed out of his suit, and the two of us drove out to the suburbs in what I'm certain Tom thought was a companionable silence. By the time we pulled up to Nina's house, I had calmed myself down.

Tom parked the car in the driveway and we walked up to the front door. There were pumpkins and gourds heaped artfully on the brick stoop, and yellow and purple mums in a huge stone pot, and shutters on every window painted a glossy forest green, and, as I stood there, in the soft glow of the antique porch light, I had a feeling that I associate with Nina Peeble, which I can only describe as a vague dissatisfaction with life. Which is not to say that I want Nina's life; that's not it. It's more that, Nina Peeble epitomizes a certain problem I have with being a woman. One of the things my mother likes to say is that women these days have too many choices. You girls have too many choices, is what she would say to my sister Meredith and me. I don't know how you're going to do it, with all these choices, she would say. And it's true, I do feel like women my age have a lot of choices. But here's my problem: nobody's choices look that good to me. And whenever I see Nina, with her house and her kid and her husband, with her garden and her projects and her dinner parties, with her casually discarded career and her perfectly toned upper arms, I see a woman who has made her choices, and she's fine with them. Not only is she fine with them, she's convinced that if you had half a brain, you'd make exactly the same ones.

The door swung open, and there was Victor, holding a margarita. Apparently it was Mexican night. He kissed me on both cheeks, and shook Tom's hand, and trailed behind us as we made our way into the kitchen.

The party was already in full swing, mostly in the kitchen. Grace, the new baby, was introduced to Tom. Drinks were offered and accepted.

"I met a guy," said Cordelia.

"Tell us about him," said Larry.

"Well, he's Canadian," said Cordelia. "And he has this way of putting his hands in his pockets."

"What can you possibly mean by that?" said Larry. He turned to Bonnie. "What can she possibly mean by that?"

Larry pressed a button on the blender and the sound of ice hitting metal blades filled the kitchen.

"I know what she means," Bonnie said when Larry was finished. "Lanky, right?"

"With oiled joints," said Cordelia. "And crow's-feet. The kind that look like they came from too much skiing."

"These are the requirements now?" said Larry. He started refilling glasses. "A Canadian who is capable of putting his hands in his pockets?"

"I don't have requirements," said Cordelia. "I don't believe in them."

"Come on," Nina said. "You must have something."

"Define 'requirements,'" said Cordelia.

Nina cocked her head to one side thoughtfully. "Non-negotiable, front-end deal-breakers."

"I don't think I do," said Cordelia.

"I don't believe you, Cordelia," said Nina. "Just like I don't believe people who say they never watch television. It sounds good, but there's simply no way that it's true."

Cordelia and Nina don't really get along. Well, that's not entirely true. Nina gets along with Cordelia all right, but Cordelia nurses all sorts of low-grade grievances against Nina of which Nina is entirely unaware. What Cordelia says about Nina is that she's self-satisfied, she's condescending, she's manipulative, and she thinks she's figured everything out. What Nina says about Cordelia is that she ought to extend her brows. Cordelia has a wideish face, and her eyebrows stop directly over the outside corners of her eyes, and Nina thinks her entire face would look different if she just penciled in another half inch or so. Nina Peeble is the kind of woman that other women spend a great deal of time thinking about, but she does not return the favor.

"I don't watch television," said Victor.

"Honey," Nina said to Victor, "you watch television. You watch baseball."

"Does that count?" said Victor.

"That's my point," said Nina. "A person can say they don't watch television, when actually they do, just like a person can say they don't have requirements, when clearly, on the face of it, they do."

"I suppose I'd have trouble with a drug addict," Cordelia said. "Or a felon."

Nina looked at Cordelia. "Well, you've been through it once already," she said. "I'm sure you're not in any hurry to do it again."

"Been through what?" said Tom.

"Marriage," said Nina.

"I don't know," said Cordelia. "I liked being married. And I like being single. What I didn't like was getting divorced. That I could have done without."

Everybody brought bowls of food into the dining room. It was Make Your Own night. Tacos, tostadas, burritos. Every so often, Larry would get up and blend a fresh batch of margaritas. The conversation tripped along nicely.

"I can't believe I forgot to tell you," Bonnie said, when we reached the public breast-feeding portion of the evening. She had angled her chair a bit away from the table and was busy trying to get Grace to latch on. "Alan and Lizzie are splitting up."

"No," said Cordelia.

"Really?" I said.

"Who are Alan and Lizzie?" said Victor.

"Bonnie's old friends from college," Nina said to him. "I met her at a shower."

"What happened?" said Cordelia.

Bonnie gave Victor a little background. Alan and Lizzie had been living together for eight years. Alan doesn't believe in marriage, and he's never been all that sure about having kids. It had been that way for as long as Lizzie had known him.

"So, they're in couple's therapy," Bonnie said. "Lizzie has given up on the idea of getting married. All she wants is to have a baby. Alan sits there each week in front of the therapist, and all he ever says is, 'you're not going to win this one.' Lizzie's crying, she's making promises like, only one baby, not two, and she'd do all the work, he wouldn't have to change a single diaper, like it was a dog she wanted to take home from the pound or something, and Alan just keeps saying to her, you're not going to win this one. That's his entire argument."

The burp cloth Bonnie had tossed over Grace's head slipped, and for a moment the table was treated to a clear view of Bonnie's enormous breast. Larry said, *"Sweetie."*

"Sorry about that," Bonnie said. She rearranged herself and then continued. "This goes on for six months. Nothing changes. Lizzie finally decides she's going to leave him. They're fighting, she's crying, and she's standing at the front door of their house with her bags packed, and the very last thing she says to him is 'I'm thirty-eight years old, we're not married, I don't have a baby — YOU WIN!'"

"Wow," said Cordelia.

I glanced at Tom. He was busy constructing one last miniature tostada.

"And she left," said Bonnie.

"Where'd she go?" I said.

"She's staying with her sister."

"Poor girl," said Cordelia.

"Well, I for one have very little sympathy for her," said Nina.

"How can you not have sympathy for her?" said Victor.

"I mean, it's sad," said Nina. "I'll give you that. But I could have told you five years ago that this is how it would end."

"You did tell me that five years ago," said Bonnie. "I just didn't believe you."

"Yes," Nina said. "I remember. You said she loved him and he loved her and it would all work out."

"What's wrong with that?" said Cordelia.

"You can't act like the rules don't apply to you," said Nina. She stood up and started to clear the plates from the table. "You can't just wake up one morning and be surprised that the man you've been living with for eight years, who refuses to marry you, who's been telling you all along that he's not sure about having kids, suddenly doesn't want to impregnate you. I mean, the woman was a fool. I'm sorry to be the one to say it, but it's true. She should have gotten out of that situation years ago."

Nina went into the kitchen with the dinner plates. Victor got up and cracked one of the windows open. He kept a pack of cigarettes on the sill, and, every night after dinner, he would perch on the ledge with his hand dangling out the window. Every so often he would hunch down, take a drag, and blow the smoke out into the cool night air.

"It's strange," said Larry. "I always thought they seemed really in love."

"Yes, well, love is not enough," Nina called out from the kitchen.

"What are you talking about?" Victor called to Nina. "It's enough for me."

Nina came back into the dining room and started getting the coffee cups out of the sideboard.

"Which is one of the things I love about you," Nina said to Victor. "You think that love is enough. But what happened with Alan and Lizzie just proves that it isn't, and the sooner two people accept that it's work and compromise and accommodation and sacrifice, the better, and the only reason to do it is because the alternative is so damn grim."

"I don't want to accept that," said Victor.

"And you don't have to, sweetheart. I do all the rest of the stuff, so you can go along in your happy little world, thinking that love is enough. But it isn't," Nina said. She put a coffee cup on its saucer with a clatter. "Love is overrated."

"Please, dear God, let us stay off the subject of sex," Victor said. "I don't want to sit at a dinner party and find out that my wife thinks sex is overrated."

Well, Nina Peeble does think sex is overrated. That is, in fact, the exact word she uses whenever you engage her on the subject. But Nina just walked up behind Victor and folded her arms across the front of his Brooks Brothers shirt and kissed him warmly on the neck.

"That," said Nina, "is something you will never, ever hear me say."

Nina went into the kitchen to get the dessert, and the conversation splintered into smaller conversations. I looked across the table at Tom. I tried to catch his eye, but he was looking down at his paper napkin, folding and refolding it. What was he thinking? How was it possible that I never had any idea what he was thinking?

I wondered if Nina was right. I wondered if love was not enough, and if the problem was that Tom and I were missing all the other stuff. The accommodation and the sacrifice. The work and the compromises. The communication and the negotiations and the counseling sessions. Then something weird started to happen to me. My heart started to pound, I felt dizzy, and, for a moment, I was certain I was going to faint. This is not hyperbole, for I am a fainter. It is the most ladylike thing about me, and even though it usually only happens in doctors' offices, it has occurred just often enough in ordinary life to remain a real threat. I closed my eyes and felt the blackness wash over me. I tried to concentrate on my breathing, on slowing down my racing heart, but I kept hearing Nina's words inside my head. Love is overrated. Love is not enough. And then, suddenly, my heart skipped a beat: maybe this *isn't* love. Maybe that's the problem. Maybe it started out as love, but somewhere, somehow, something happened to it, and it became something else.

I want the big love. I opened my eyes and looked over at Tom. He was still busy with the napkin. *And I am not going to find it here.* I saw it with a shimmering clarity. It didn't matter that I could finally see that there are worse things in life than having a person sleep with somebody else when they're supposed to be sleeping with only you, there are worse things than not knowing, there are worse things than being humiliated. It didn't matter that I was almost thirty-three, or that my eggs were curdling inside of me, or that there were no men left in Philadelphia, there were no men left anywhere, except maybe in Alaska, which meant I'd have to go to Alaska for a man and to China for a baby, which meant a lot of time on the Internet, and long-haul flights, neither of which I'm particularly fond of. None of it mattered. The only thing that mattered was that this wasn't love. It wasn't the big love. And I realized that I could spend the rest of my life trying to hold on to Tom. I could do my best to cement him in place. I could work hard to convince him that he couldn't live without me. But I suddenly saw that I had another option. I could just let go. And, just like that, I could feel something shifting inside me, something that had been a certain way as long as I could remember.

All of this was so startling, really, that I felt like I was waking up from a dream. I realize that's a terrible cliché, but that's exactly what it felt like. I shook my head, and then I looked across the table at Tom, and it was like I was seeing him for the first time. He was leaning back in his chair so he could talk to Victor, who was still perched on the windowsill. They were talking about mortgage rates. The light from one of the wall sconces hit the back of Tom's head, and his blond hair glowed. I always loved Tom's hair. Whenever I ran though the features I wanted our children to inherit, I'd always mix things up a bit to keep it interesting, but that part never changed; the hair was always his. The nose was always mine and the hair was always his.

"I think," I said to no one in particular, "that love should be enough."

"What's that?" said Larry.

"I think, love should be enough," I said, quite loudly this time.

"Run away with me, Alison," Victor said to me. He blew a large cloud of smoke into the dining room. "We can be romantics together."

"I've never been a romantic before," I said. "But I'm thinking of becoming one."

I looked at Tom.

"I think it's time to go," I said.

Twenty-two

TOM AND I WERE OVER THAT NIGHT. IT WAS ALL VERY GROWN up and very final. I felt I owed him that much. I left first thing the next morning and moved in with Cordelia. The plan was that I would find a new job and then get my own apartment.

"To your new life," said Cordelia, clinking my glass.

"To my new life," I said.

When Cordelia came home from the gym the next day, I was lying in her bed in the fetal position.

"I thought you said you were fine with this," said Cordelia.

"I am fine with it," I said.

She sat down on the bed next to me.

"Conceptually," I said.

She nodded her head.

"I just need to catch up with myself," I said.

By Monday, all the shades were down, and I had moved the

television in from the other room and put it on top of a trunk at the foot of the bed. I was propped up with pillows against the headboard, listlessly flipping through the channels.

"I don't understand people who say there's nothing to watch on TV," I said to Cordelia when she came home from work.

Cordelia walked across the room and cracked open a window.

"My theory," I continued, "is that people who say there's nothing to watch on TV don't watch enough TV."

Cordelia bent down and picked up a few stray magazines and put them back on the nightstand.

"There's a whole world in there," I said.

And so I retired to Cordelia's bed for a while. I must say, she handled it exceedingly well. Her mother had shut herself up in a darkened second-floor bedroom for most of the seventies, so my behavior didn't alarm her nearly as much as it might have. She mashed me potatoes and scrambled me eggs. She brought me my favorite sick snack — Saltine crackers and blueberry jam — and didn't even flinch when a blob of blueberries landed on her duvet. I can't remember much of what we talked about. I do remember thinking, while Cordelia was rubbing my feet with peppermint lotion one evening, that I was beginning to understand why Cordelia's mother found it so appealing to stay in bed for months at a time. I never would have put up with myself.

I lay there for hours, for entire days, going over all that had happened between Tom and me, churning it through my brain. I circled around to the same thought again and again. When I was sitting in the cab, flipping through my desk calendar, trying to figure out whose hypothetical child I was carrying, what had happened was this: I kept picturing Henry's ears. On the baby's head. Then, very deliberately, I had put the thought out of my mind. I was with Tom. Tom's ears were fine. But lying in bed at Cordelia's, I kept coming back to that moment, and, in a weird way, it made me feel better. I wasn't supposed to wake up next to those ears for the rest of my life. The truth is, I didn't *want* to spend my life with those ears. And something inside me had known it, even if it took the rest of me a while to catch up.

"I think I'm depressed," I finally said to Cordelia.

"You're molting," she said kindly.

"I want to die," I said.

"You're in your cocoon," said Cordelia.

"I can't move my limbs," I said.

"That's what happens in a cocoon," she said. "Limbs don't move."

And then one morning I opened my eyes, and all I could see were the dust motes sparkling in the sunlight, and I knew I was done with that. The molting, I mean. I got out of bed and took a shower. I put on my running shoes and went for a run. I called up a temp agency. The woman I met with knew me from my column, and she quickly found me a truly plum job, in the temp world at least, copyediting at an advertising agency in place of a woman on an extended maternity leave. ("Triplets. At forty," the temp lady reported when she phoned with the offer. "Fertility drugs, anyone?") I cut off most of my hair, which turned out to be a mistake, but I also accidentally lost seven pounds, so I ended up about even.

The first apartment I looked at was just down the street from

Cordelia's. It was cheap and tiny and, to my eyes, perfect. The windows were huge and the late-afternoon light poured in, and it was just high up enough to give a sort of Mary Poppins perspective of rooftops and chimneys and the tops of really tall trees. Nina Peeble came apartment hunting with me that day, and while I swooned around the windows, she wrinkled her nose at the avocado-colored bathroom tile and the two puny closets and said, "You can't live in a view, Alison." Well, I thought about it and decided that I could. So now I live in a view.

And I started to get that feeling, that great feeling, where the world starts opening up again, where you notice a flier for Italian lessons stuck to a lamppost, and you pull off the little tag with the phone number and slip it in your wallet, and when you come upon the tag again a week later you impulsively make the call, and you end up spending two hours every Wednesday night with six strangers in the back of a café being drilled by Alessandro, who wears leather pants and calls you *Principessa* when he talks to you after class. You know the feeling I'm talking about. Life, which had shrunk down to mundane and predictable proportions, suddenly exploded with, well, *life*. I bought lacy bras and hiking boots. I kept Keats on the back of the toilet and decided it was time to finally tackle Proust. I pored over the travel section of the Sunday *Times* with the intensity of a person who believes that anything, anywhere, is possible. I went to the opera and I took up yoga and I taught myself how to make a chocolate soufflé.

I have not yet been able to get this particular feeling when I'm involved with somebody. I've just never been able to manage it.

I mean, I *do* things when I'm involved with somebody — I go shopping and I cook things, I take trips and I read books — but somehow the enterprise is never fueled by the sense that my life could, at any moment, turn out to be something entirely different than I had anticipated. It is a problem. It is one of the major problems of my life. I'm sure there's a reason for it — an explanation for why life opens up and closes down around a person — and I started to develop a theory about it, but then I stopped. And I've simply decided to fight it. To stop shrinking down. To keep on unfolding, no matter what.

A few months after I moved into my new apartment, something quite unexpected happened. I remember thinking at the time that I wasn't sure if it was the ending of this story or the beginning of a new one. It was late on a Sunday afternoon, and I was poking around in the map store on Chestnut Street, looking at travel books. I heard a voice behind me.

"Alison?"

I turned around. It was Henry.

"Hello," I said.

He leaned forward and gave me an awkward kiss on the cheek.

"How are you?" said Henry.

"I'm good," I said. "How are you?"

"Hanging in there," said Henry.

"I heard you quit the paper."

"Quit. Got fired," said Henry. "I think the distinction becomes meaningless when both parties are screaming profanities down a long hallway."

"You yelled at Sid?" I said.

"I did."

"I wish I'd yelled," I said.

"We got a bunch of letters about you," said Henry. "Protesting your departure."

I looked at him. "Define a bunch."

"Okay," said Henry. "Six. But you have six extremely loyal, angry fans."

"Tell me about what's-her-face," I said, "that girl who stole my job."

"Mary Ellen?" said Henry. "What do you want to know?"

"I don't know," I said. "Just say some bad things about her."

"Well, she can't write," said Henry.

"Yeah. Stuff like that."

"And she bites the heads off of kittens."

"Give me one more," I said.

"Deep down, she's an insecure, unhappy person," said Henry. "It's sad, really."

"You know, I hate that sort of thing."

"What sort of thing?"

"The idea that being insecure and unhappy is an excuse for anything," I said. "I mean, I'm insecure and unhappy. Everybody I *know* is insecure and unhappy."

"You're absolutely right," said Henry. "She's just a plain old bad person."

"And untalented," I said.

"Hugely untalented."

Henry smiled.

"What?" I said.

"Nothing," said Henry.

"Why are you smiling?"

"I don't know," said Henry. "I'm just smiling."

"What are you going to do now?" I said.

"I'm not sure," he said. "Take a break. Reassess things."

He showed me the stack of Lonely Planet guidebooks he was holding — Thailand, Nepal, Cambodia, and Tibet.

"I told the guy behind the counter that I wanted to go someplace cheap, where people wear long orange robes," said Henry. "Apparently I need to narrow it down further."

"Do you want mountains and trekking or beaches and whores?" I said.

He sighed a big mock sigh. "I guess trekking."

I took the Thailand and Cambodia guides out of his stack and put them back on the shelf. "There," I said. "You're narrowed."

"Are you going someplace?"

I nodded. "Italy. In two weeks."

"Why Italy?" said Henry.

I decided to tell him the truth. "It's a reward for not sleeping with my Italian teacher."

Henry laughed.

"He was, I don't know," I said. "Creepy sexy. And I was intrigued. But then I realized that the sexy part was the Italian part, and the creepy part was just him."

Henry asked if I wanted to get a cup of coffee. I said yes. We each bought our books, and then we went around the corner to a tiny café. We sat for a long time, talking.

By the time we left, it was dark outside. Henry grabbed my hand as we crossed the street against the light, and when we got to the other side, he didn't let go.

It was a clear night, and the moon was full and bright and low in the sky. I didn't know where we were going, but it didn't matter, because the cherry blossoms were finally out, and the air smelled of the last fire in somebody's fireplace. I just wanted to stare at the moon. I just wanted to lift my face to that moon, unashamed, like a sunflower to the sun.